Around the Next Bend

RASPBERRY RIDGE
BOOK FOUR

JESSIE GUSSMAN

Contents

Acknowledgments • v

Chapter 1 • 1
Chapter 2 • 9
Chapter 3 • 19
Chapter 4 • 23
Chapter 5 • 32
Chapter 6 • 38
Chapter 7 • 44
Chapter 8 • 50
Chapter 9 • 57
Chapter 10 • 66
Chapter 11 • 73
Chapter 12 • 78
Chapter 13 • 86
Chapter 14 • 94
Chapter 15 • 98
Chapter 16 • 101
Chapter 17 • 110
Chapter 18 • 117
Chapter 19 • 125
Chapter 20 • 134
Chapter 21 • 140
Chapter 22 • 145
Epilogue • 149

Sneak Peek of Into the Golden Dawn • 153
Read More Jessie! • 161
A Gift from Jessie • 163
Escape to more faith-filled romance series by Jessie Gussman! • 165

Acknowledgments

Cover art by Julia Gussman
Editing by Heather Hayden
Narration by Jay Dyess
Author Services by CE Author Assistant

Listen to the unabridged audio for FREE performed by Jay Dyess on the Say with Jay channel on YouTube. Get early access to all of Jay's recordings and listen to Jessie's books before they're available to the general public, plus get daily Bible readings by Jay and bonus scenes by becoming a Say with Jay channel member.

One

This might have been the biggest mistake of his life.

"We're looking forward to hearing you speak tomorrow, Garnet," Mrs. Brandstetter said as she shook his hand. Her husband, Mr. Brandstetter, stood silently behind her, looking stern and serious. As he should.

Picking any pastor was not something that should be done on a whim. But a small-town church, especially one in a town as tiny as Raspberry Ridge, presented its own set of problems. The least of which was whether or not the church was going to be able to pay the pastor's salary.

Garnet still wasn't sure that was actually going to happen. The pastoral committee had warned him that he was going to need to retain his full-time job even after they voted him in.

Garnet didn't tell them that he had already given his two-week notice and his last day was yesterday. He'd spent years going to Bible school around a full-time job, studying, learning and finally receiving a degree from a respected school in pastoral studies. He'd been ordained in his denomination and had served as an unpaid assistant pastor in his church in Indiana, before leaving it all behind. It wasn't a spur of the moment decision. He truly believed the Lord wanted him here, and not just for the church.

His eyes drifted to his daughter, Dabney, fourteen years old and not very happy to be pulled out of the homeschool they had been a part of on the other side of the Michigan line, in Indiana, and to be moved two hundred miles away to the small town of Raspberry Ridge. The fact that it was directly beside Lake Michigan, and she'd basically be almost living in a beach house, had made the move only marginally better. Dabney, while mature for her age, was still a typical fourteen-year-old, and her life revolved around her friends.

The fact that he had homeschooled her from the very beginning, and that the "school" she was leaving there was the homeschool co-op where she had grown up with other homeschooled children, didn't matter to a teen. Moving was moving.

She sat outside the window, on one of the church benches overlooking the wide expanse of Lake Michigan, with a book in her hand, her head bent, her legs tucked up around her.

She must have inherited her father's personality, since her mother was a real go-getter. Nothing stood in Mertie's way when Mertie wanted to get something, not even the inconvenience of a child.

Garnet smiled at the next person who waited to shake his hand. He wanted to make a good impression on the pastoral committee, even though they'd already voted to allow him to come candidate. He would preach two Sundays in a row, and then the church would vote on whether or not they wanted to retain him.

He didn't want to think about Mertie, but how could he not? She had been his best friend as they'd grown up in Raspberry Ridge. And when she'd come to him asking for his help, he hadn't been able to turn her down.

But he also hadn't been able to do what she wanted him to do.

Because of that, he hadn't been able to see her since. And he wasn't sure seeing her now was such a good idea. He hadn't expected her to be back in town to close up and sell the mansion her parents had left to her and her sisters when they had been tragically killed in a car accident earlier in the year.

"Welcome to Raspberry Ridge." Homer Aiken stood in front of him, his hand out. Homer had impressed him as an intelligent man with a discernment for truth and a desire to do right. He had been slow to speak and always quick to listen.

"Thank you. It's good to be back in my hometown."

He and Homer hadn't grown up together, although they knew each other. Homer was a good bit younger than Garnet.

"I've been leading a Bible study on my front porch at seven o'clock every morning. Even on Sundays, since there is no church. I...haven't talked it over with the people who've been attending, but I think we'd be honored to have you attend, and if you'd like to lead it, it would be even better."

Garnet appreciated this gesture of hospitality. In his experience, small towns were notoriously difficult to assimilate in. A person always felt like an outsider. Even after they'd been there for forty years. The small town he lived in in northern Indiana had been exactly like that. People had accepted him, they'd been kind to him, but they'd always considered him an outsider.

Of course, Raspberry Ridge was his hometown, although he'd been away for years.

"I'd love to," he said immediately. If they were going to ask him, he was going to do it. He had quit his day job in order to move back to Raspberry Ridge. He hadn't really enjoyed the sales position that he had at the company he worked for since he moved to Indiana and wasn't going to miss the little cubicle and monotonous workday, followed by as much time as he could get with his daughter.

It had been hard to squeeze in the time he needed to homeschool her since he'd been promoted from his administrative position four years ago. Back then, he had worked from home, and his hours were flexible.

"We've been reading through the Bible, and we're in the book of Deuteronomy, chapter 10, but you can teach from wherever you want. My wife and I started the Bible study when she said she wanted to know what the Bible said but had never read it through. So, we typically read a few chapters and talk about them. Sometimes we get through one, sometimes more than that. I usually have Matthew Henry's commentary and maybe a few other resources I pull up on my phone."

"Thanks for the heads-up. I'm happy to do it, and I'll just continue doing what you do. I'll get a few things together so I can say a few words about that chapter and possibly up to four others." It felt good to be given a job. To have something concrete in front of him to do.

He did have the blog that he had been working on building for the last ten years. Blogs had not quite gone the way of rotary phones, but they weren't as profitable as they had been in their heyday.

He'd also been working on starting a TikTok channel, but in his experience, people on TikTok weren't exactly interested in God's word. Maybe he just hadn't found his people yet, or maybe it was a mission field and he should keep working on it. God hadn't shown him for sure, yet.

He shook the hand of the next person in line, nodded as they welcomed him, speaking some words about how they were looking forward to hearing him speak on Sunday. He responded and tried to project confidence.

Lord, I'm trusting this is the right thing to do. I was sure this was all Your plan, but now that I'm here, I feel lost and a little nervous. Please don't let Dabney suffer because I made a mistake.

That summed up his years of being a dad. Everything that he did, he did with Dabney in mind.

Of course, he always had to follow the Lord's leading, but it was always with an eye toward his daughter.

Lord, You know I had no idea that Mertie was in town.

He broke off with that thought. It had been in his mind that he needed to avoid her at all costs. As much as he didn't want to. Over the years, it had gotten easier, and sometimes he even almost forgot about her. Although with Dabney in his home, it was almost impossible, since she was a carbon copy of her mother. In her features, anyway. Personality wise, she couldn't have been more different.

Garnet had always appreciated the fact that God had given him a laid-back, easygoing daughter who had never been demanding, even as a baby. Her toddler years had been a dream. He watched as other parents had struggled with their children, temper tantrums and attitude were common, and at times, Garnet was tempted to believe it was his parenting skills that had kept Dabney from going down the same road, but he knew better.

He had no idea how to be a parent and had flown by the seat of his pants, reading as many books as he could on the subject and occasionally going back to talk to his parents.

Being that the only child his parents had raised was him, they weren't a lot of help, although, according to them, he had been as easy as Dabney.

Until this point, though, he had tried to avoid being in Raspberry Ridge as much as he possibly could without being obvious about it. He hadn't wanted to run into Mertie. Although from what he'd seen, she hadn't gone back much, if at all.

So what were the odds that he felt the Lord had led him to come back for good, and she was here?

"Looking forward to seeing what you do with the church. I'm just as excited as the rest of the town to have it open again. It's perfect timing for us," Hobert Gilcrest spoke as he shook Garnet's hand.

Hobert had told Garnet that he and his fiancée were interested in getting married. They intended to build a small house down by the dock where Hobert kept his boat and start a family.

Coincidentally, or maybe not so much so, Hobert's fiancée was Mertie's sister. Amara recognized him, knew him, but did not realize that Dabney was her sister's child.

Thankfully, Dabney was always happy to sit somewhere with her nose in a book, and while people had met her, she hadn't hung around. As far as Garnet knew, Amara had not looked Dabney full in the face. If she had, there was no way she wouldn't see the family resemblance.

Nervousness tightened his muscles, and he had to deliberately relax his face into a smile.

"I love it when God's timing works that way," he said, meaning it. Obviously Hobert and Amara were starting a family here in Raspberry Ridge, and having a church, not just where they could hear the preaching of the word several times a week, but also where they could go to enjoy fellowship with their church family, would be helpful in keeping them on the straight and narrow, raising their family for God's glory.

"I appreciate the fact that you know the importance of the church and intend to include that in your daily life. It's encouraging to me," Garnet said, knowing that he sounded serious and possibly even boring. People had accused him of that. He wasn't quite sure how he had been able to become a good salesperson. After all, most of the top salespeople were jovial people pleasers with the ability to talk to anyone and with a joke always on the ready.

Garnet was pretty much the opposite of all that. But maybe it was his reliability. The way people seemed to be able to look at him and feel like he was honest and trustworthy. He just had a way about him, people said, that made them think that whatever he was saying was the absolute truth.

As well they should, since he made it a point to always speak the truth.

"Welcome to Raspberry Ridge. I'm confident that our little congregation is going to love you, and you're going to be a part of it for a long time. Of course, you have some big shoes to fill."

Dominic Miller stood in front of him shaking his hand. Dominic was the head deacon and the leader of the small pastoral committee. He was the one that Garnet needed to impress, not that Garnet was keeping track or making an effort to be anything other than himself. He was just going to be who he was and allow the Lord to work things out. At least, that was his plan. Sometimes things didn't go according to plan, but God had the ability to straighten anything out.

"Pastor Calvin was a good man. You know he was my preacher throughout my growing-up years. He definitely shaped my personality and my thinking. I am forever indebted to him for preaching solely from the Bible and not trying to slant his sermons to preach what he wanted to say or support his political opinions."

Very few people did that anymore. They took out the things they didn't like or ignored them. And then put in things that suited their social narrative. That was part of the reason Garnet had decided to become a minister. People didn't know what the Bible said anymore.

And yet, how could they be Christians if they didn't know what a Christian was? What a Christian was supposed to do?

The questions had bothered him, until he finally realized that God was prompting him, Garnet Irving, to become a preacher of the word.

> *How beautiful upon the mountains are the feet of*
> *him that bringeth good tidings, that*
> *publisheth peace; that bringeth good tidings of*
> *good, that publisheth salvation; that saith*
> *unto Zion, Thy God reigneth!*

He remembered quite clearly the day he'd read that verse and realized that God wasn't just prompting him to study more, He was prompting him to study so that he could teach others.

Sometimes the idea that God was using him, a studious kid from a small town—so small it didn't even have a stoplight—in Michigan, to spread the gospel to his people, still brought Garnet up short.

But there was also the verse that said that a pastor should be the husband of one wife.

That verse could be interpreted to mean that a pastor should only have one wife - that he shouldn't be divorced and remarried or polygamous. Or it could indicate that a pastor should be married. He chose to believe it meant that he needed a wife. After all, God created him to need a help meet. Others might disagree, and he would not say they were wrong, but he was not going to take a pastorate without a wife.

Lord, You said if I go, You would provide what I need. I can't be a pastor if I don't have a wife. It's right there in Your word.

He and God had been having this conversation for a while. Garnet had been listening as well as he could, knowing that God sometimes didn't move until the last minute. But Garnet had determined in his heart that he would not accept the pastorate on a permanent basis if he did not have a wife.

You're cutting things a little close, Lord.

He figured that's the way Daniel must have felt, when he got thrown in the lion's den. Perhaps it was the way Shadrach, Meshach, and Abednego felt when they had been put in the fiery furnace. He thought about other men through history who must have wondered at God's timing and whether God was really going to come through. But a person's faith couldn't be tested if God did everything on the human timeframe, because if it had been up to Garnet, he would have had a wife fifteen years ago.

Two

Mertie wiped the sweat from her brow as she moved the stiff bristle brush across the outside light fixture, scrubbing off the bird dirt, the cobwebs, and anything else that had attached itself to the siding over the years.

This house was going to shine, gleam, be a beckoning light on a hill, a home the prospective owners would absolutely not be able to resist, and it would get snapped up immediately, the second it went on the market.

Mertie was determined that would happen. She did not have time to sit around and wait for the house to be on the market for six, eight months, a year. She didn't even want it to be on the market for two months. So she had a goal—four weeks from now, the entire house would be spotless, totally cleaned out, and ready to be shown to prospective buyers.

She intended that it be put on the market and sell that very day.

She was known for setting goals and achieving them.

That was why she had been up at five o'clock in the morning, scrubbing the outside of the place.

It was 6:30, and her stomach was rumbling, reminding her that all she had was a cup of coffee this morning, and it was time for breakfast.

"Are you coming to Bible study with me this morning?" Her sister, Amara, had walked out of the door and stood with her Bible tucked under her arm, a mug of coffee, lid firmly attached, in her other hand.

"No. Not today." Not ever if she could help it. She would work, spending all of her free time getting the house ready.

"But the new preacher is going to be doing it today. And considering your line of work, I would think that you would be interested. People are interested in your opinion of him."

"Well, they can be interested all they want to, as much as I hate to turn down Bible study." She did love studying God's word, and she loved studying God's word with other Christians, but not in Raspberry Ridge. There were too many memories here. Too many things she wanted to forget. She didn't want to stay here any longer than she had to. When she had arrived yesterday afternoon, she and Amara had gone over all the things that they needed to do, and she had determined that she was going to start and not quit until they were done. That included stopping for Bible study.

Are you too busy for me? Are you being a Martha in a world where you should be a Mary?

Mertie's hands stilled, although she gripped the brush tightly, closing her eyes.

Over the years, she'd gotten better at hearing God's still, small voice. She was a go-getter; she got things done. She saw black and white and was easily able to discern between truth and lie, right and wrong, good and evil.

That is part of why she had become a successful Christian speaker and author, in demand all across the country. She wasn't quite in the top tier of Christian speakers, but she was getting there. There were only a few men who were bigger than she was, and they all had churches. She, of course, was not a pastor, because the Bible expressly said a pastor should be the husband of one wife. Considering that she would never be a husband, she could not be a pastor. Plus, the Bible also said it was a shame for women to speak in church.

She didn't write the Bible, she just tried to live it. But she refused to try to explain the parts she didn't like away or decide to ignore the stuff she wished wasn't there. Sometimes it made her mad, and she'd had more than one conversation with the Lord about it. But she was reminded of the passage in Judges where Deborah was chosen to lead the Israelites because there wasn't a man who wanted to do it. It was a shame for men.

Somehow, God, when He created humanity, had decided which jobs were best suited for which genders, and He had handed those jobs out. Who was she to question Him? She couldn't make a world. She couldn't even make a blade of grass grow. She couldn't create one single-celled organism, let alone the whole planet full of them. She supposed, when she was able to do those things, then she could decide that women could be pastors.

In her line of work, sometimes she met people who got angry about it, but the Bible didn't say that women couldn't make just as good pastors as men. God just gave women different jobs. She could either follow God and His Word, or she could make her own way, but then it would be her religion and not really a Christian way. And as much as she had a commanding personality, with a full-steam-ahead attitude, she truly did want to submit to God and obey. Even though it wasn't what she would have chosen if she had been writing the Bible.

Regardless, she recognized that voice and knew that her choice to work instead of going to Bible study was not the right one.

"Amara?" she said, calling after her sister who was halfway down the walk.

"Yeah?" Amara said cheerfully, stopping and turning, lifting her coffee to her lips and taking a small sip.

"Hold on a second. I... I'm a mess, but let me grab my Bible and a cup of coffee." She was going to need another cup, since she wasn't going to get breakfast for at least an hour. More likely an hour and half, or two. Depending on how long everyone wanted to talk.

Maybe, if she was lucky, it would be one of those Bible studies where someone was assigned to bring food.

She didn't even care if it was good. Just something to put in her empty belly. She wasn't used to getting up and working for an hour and a half before breakfast.

But if that was what needed to be done, that's what she would do.

She climbed down off the ladder and hurried into the house, going upstairs and grabbing her Bible on her nightstand where she had read a few verses and prayed this morning, intending to have a longer time of devotions in the afternoon when she was ready for a break from work. She often taught in her books and speeches that it didn't matter when a person got into the Bible, just a matter that they did.

Of course, the Bible itself said morning, noon, and night will I pray, so, for her, morning, noon, and night was the standard.

Regardless, she grabbed her Bible, and the notebook that was never far from it, and hurried back down the stairs, glancing in the mirror as she went out of her room and sighing a little. Mertie Jardine, speaker, writer, and teacher of the Bible, was not exactly put together this morning. She had a handkerchief tied around her hair, dirt splatters on her face, and she wore the oldest clothes in her wardrobe, clothes she had pulled out of the closet that had belonged to her sister back in the day. Old jeans with holes in both knees and a T-shirt so thin a person could almost see through it, the logo long since faded away, although she thought it might have been for the Michigan Wolverines, but wasn't sure.

Regardless, her ratty old tennis shoes completed the look, and no one would look at her picture on her book jackets and confuse that woman with the woman who was walking out of the house, coffee in hand, clutching her Bible right now.

"I'm so glad you're coming," Amara said, a big smile on her face.

The smile was probably less about Mertie going and more about the man who was walking up the drive to meet them. Hobert Gilcrest had asked her sister to marry him, and they were hoping to get the new pastor to do the ceremony soon. Preferably, right after he was ordained in the church. Mertie had heard nothing but good things about the man candidating for the pastor position, although she hadn't caught his name.

She just knew it was a man and that he had a daughter.

Which led Mertie to wonder if he might be married and divorced, since she had heard nothing about a wife.

She hadn't worried about it though. It wasn't her town, and he wasn't going to be her pastor. She had a small home in the suburbs of Chicago, which she used as her base when she wasn't traveling, which she did as much as she could. She did not turn down a request, although she had blocked out the next four weeks in her schedule to help her sisters get their parents' house ready for market.

"I've heard he's really good," Mertie said, tucking her hand in Amara's elbow, as they walked toward Hobert.

"I'm sure he is. I trust the opinion of the pastoral committee."

"Anyone who wants to come here to preach would have to be preaching for the sake of the gospel and not for filthy lucre." She said "filthy lucre" with a little bit of irony, since that was the phrase the Bible used. Her sister would recognize that even though it might not be something that even a casual Christian would recognize.

It was nice to be among people who understood her and got her humor. Especially since she wasn't exactly known as a humorous person. Of course, a teacher of the Bible probably was expected to be serious and studious and look like a trustworthy person. Mertie had never had to work on that. It had come naturally. Although, keeping secrets, hiding a part of herself, didn't come naturally, and there was one big secret that she kept, always.

As they walked, they met Hobert, and she stepped back a bit as Amara and Hobert embraced, smiling at each other and whispering a few words as they exchanged a kiss.

A little part of Mertie's heart squeezed. She had determined that a romantic relationship was not something that she would pursue, ever. She had messed up, and while she didn't believe in penance, she did believe in reaping what a person sowed, and she had sowed something terrible in her youth. And what she was going to reap was giving up any idea of a romantic, lifetime relationship. Even though she wanted it. What person didn't want to have a life partner standing beside them through the trials and tribulations of this earthly journey?

Soon they were back on their way, and it didn't take long to walk down the driveway. They nodded and waved to several people on the sidewalk as they walked up the street to Homer's and Skyler's house. It was the last house on the street, before the healing garden and the bluffs, below which there was a pebble beach, where she and her sisters had spent many a summer afternoon swimming and dreaming.

That was before their parents had moved them to Chicago and her life had taken a screeching left turn.

Since adulthood, she'd only been back once, and that had been for something she never talked about.

There were several people already gathered on the porch, and when they saw Mertie and Amara and Hobert coming, someone jumped up to go get more chairs.

There was a small table set up, with a breakfast casserole sitting on it, along with plates and plastic forks. It was already more than half gone.

"Help yourself to some casserole. We already prayed," a smiling, very pregnant woman said.

She thought it might be Vera Miller. She had been around town when Mertie had grown up, but that had been more than ten years ago.

Hobert cut a piece for Amara and himself, and they walked off, leaving Mertie to cut her own.

They were so cute together, talking softly and exchanging sweet smiles. Mertie was happy for Amara, even though she thought Amara might be a little off her rocker to have given up such a prestigious and lucrative job in Chicago to become the wife of a fisherman in a tiny town that no one had ever heard of.

Still, Mertie was not going to judge. If that was the Lord's will for her, then that's what her sister should do. Sometimes it was hard to remember that money wasn't everything, although Mertie understood the temptation. And she admired her sister for understanding that and choosing the better thing.

Mertie tucked a stray piece of hair underneath the kerchief she had on her head and then picked up the plate where she'd plopped a small piece of breakfast casserole. She was starving, but as a public speaker who was constantly in the public eye, she couldn't afford to eat as much as she wanted to. She needed to stay slim. Even though she was a Christian speaker, and she was supposed to be speaking to people who looked at your heart and not the way you looked on the outside, it was still imperative that she keep her figure slim and trim. No one wanted to see someone on stage who didn't look their best.

Plus, she could hardly teach about moderation, if she didn't practice it herself.

Taking her piece of casserole to the porch steps, she didn't wait for a chair, but stepped down two steps, and sat down. There was a man on a chair right at the top of the steps, his feet stretched out and crossed, his Bible in his lap and a pen in his hand as he made a note on a small notebook he had on one knee.

He looked up casually as she walked by and nodded a greeting.

He looked familiar, the same way Vera Miller looked familiar. Probably someone she had known twenty years ago but didn't recognize now.

She wasn't going to be in town long, and as the man looked right back down at his notebook, she didn't introduce herself but took a seat on the second step down and said a silent prayer over her casserole before she began to eat.

She assumed the eating happened before the teaching, maybe so the casserole wouldn't get cold or to give people time to wander in.

Someone came out with more chairs, and a couple more people arrived, while Mertie finished her casserole and opened her Bible to Deuteronomy ten, which she had overheard in a conversation above her head would be the starting place for them today.

"Good morning, Connie," an older woman said as she gingerly sat down on the step by Mertie's knee, calling her by her mother's name.

"Good morning. And Connie is actually my mother. I'm Mertie. Her oldest daughter."

The woman's eyes, a little rheumy and confused, narrowed as her brows drew down.

"You couldn't be. She didn't have children," she said, sounding like she knew exactly what she was talking about.

"She has Alzheimer's." The man above her spoke softly, for her ears only.

Mertie didn't even look up but just lifted her head, acknowledging his words and thinking about how familiar his voice sounded before she looked back at the woman.

"Of course. My mistake," she said, keeping herself from saying "my bad" at the last moment. The woman probably wouldn't understand the modern-day slang.

"This is my mother, Gertie." Homer came over, offering her coffee, lifting up the pot he held in a silent question.

She shook her head. Too much coffee and she got exceptionally hyper. She had to limit her intake.

"I remember Gertie," she said fondly, thinking about the woman who had always had a cookie to offer her after school or a cold drink of lemonade on a hot summer day when they were walking down to the pebble beach.

It was sad that she was suffering from Alzheimer's, and it made Mertie feel a nostalgic homesickness that she hadn't felt in forever.

Of course, she couldn't remember those days without thinking of Garnet and how they had been inseparable until her family had moved away. He had been her best friend since she was old enough to remember having friends. Her sisters had tagged along when she and Garnet had allowed it, but they always seemed rather immature and young.

Garnet and she had ridden their bikes together, climbed the bluffs together, and swum in the lake together. They had been allowed to swim as long as they had a buddy, and she and Garnet were each other's buddies.

Of course, she couldn't think of Garnet without remembering that last fateful time that she had seen him, seeing the disappointment in his eyes and hearing him ask her if she would do the one thing she knew she couldn't.

Through the years, every once in a while she would wonder what would have happened if she would have said yes. But she had made a different decision. And she never allowed herself to look back with regret. Just kept her eyes forward and concentrated on what God wanted her to do.

Gertie was rambling on about something that her mother would probably know exactly what she was talking about, but Mertie had no idea so she just nodded and tried to say things that would not set the older lady off.

Finally, after about ten minutes of chatting and finishing up their breakfast casserole, the man above her cleared his throat and said, "I think it's about time for us to get started. And I wanted to thank you all for coming. Maybe you were expecting Homer to be leading us today, but Homer asked me to, since I am candidating at the church, and he thought it would give everyone a chance to hear me a little more." The man's voice held humor, like he wasn't sure why anyone would want to hear him more, and Mertie liked the confident way he spoke, while still allowing a bit of humor in his tone.

As he spoke, her eyes were caught on a young teenaged girl who had been sitting on a tire swing in the front yard. As the man spoke, she had closed her book, got off the swing, and started walking slowly through the yard, picking her Bible and notebook up from where they sat on the ground near the sidewalk.

She started to make her way toward the porch while the man mentioned that he had grown up in Raspberry Ridge and had moved in with his parents, who were getting older and needed and appreciated him coming back to give them a hand with the yard work and upkeep on their big old, empty house.

"And some of you already know that I have a daughter. Her name is Dabney, and she'll be joining us, because she wants to, not because I'm making her," he said, and that humor was back. Mertie heard it in his voice as his daughter lifted her eyes, and Mertie found herself looking into eyes that were the exact same shade of blue as her own.

As her eyes roved over the girl's face, she realized the features were very familiar as well. Even the hair color was the same as hers.

It couldn't be.

"Oh," the man above her said. "I guess I should start out with my name. For those of you who haven't been talking to the pastoral committee, I'm Garnet Irving. And I'm here to candidate to be the new preacher at the Raspberry Ridge Bible Church."

Mertie felt the world tilt and sway, and she put a hand beside her, grabbing the banister, taking a deep breath, trying to clear her head.

Garnet Irving.

No wonder the man's voice had sounded so familiar, no wonder he had looked familiar, it was Garnet.

She didn't say a word to anyone, simply grasped her notebook and Bible in one hand, her coffee cup in the other, jumped up, and hurried off the steps, all but running down the sidewalk and fleeing headlong into the healing garden. Knowing that if she ran home, everyone on the porch would be able to see her the entire way, and only wanting to get away from the prying eyes and out of the presence of the one person who knew her deepest, darkest secret: Garnet Irving.

Three

Garnet watched Mertie hurry away. He recognized her immediately when she had come up on the porch. It was no surprise that she might not recognize him. Back when she had known him, his cheeks had been as smooth as hers, and now, while he didn't quite have a full beard, there were three or four days' worth of stubble on them, and his voice had certainly deepened, not that he spoke much to her. He couldn't help but help her out when Gertie had sat down beside her and insisted that she was her mother. It was easy to understand when one knew that Gertie was dealing with Alzheimer's. Then her odd conversation made sense.

He had wanted to talk to her, had wanted to open up a conversation, tell her how happy he was to see her, ask her if she might want to see her daughter, but he should have known better. He had followed her career. He knew she was a rising star in the Christian speaker and writer industry, and she was paying her dues, almost ready to break out into big time.

He wouldn't be the slightest bit surprised if she had her own TV show. She certainly had written books that were very popular and had her own podcast as well. Her speaking schedule stretched far into next year and, as far as he could tell, was completely sold out.

Of course he didn't really know what to say to her. He was nowhere near as successful as she was, as the world defined success. He was simply doing what God wanted him to do, taking the pastorate of the church with less than twenty-five members. It wasn't going to support him; the small amount that they were able to pay was definitely not going to support him and his daughter, and the amount of money that he was making from his social media presence, and the one book that he had written, would barely pay for groceries.

None of that mattered, as he watched the woman disappear into the healing garden, the quiet on the porch almost louder than the pair of fighter jets that passed overhead.

As the leader of the group that morning, he should say something, but Garnet didn't know what to say. He could hardly say, "Hey, it's my fault she left. She heard my name, and I know something about her that no one else in the world knows, and it would ruin her ministry if it came out." Or at least, she would think it would. That was her main concern back when she had brought the child to him, that it was going to destroy everything she was building toward. Even back then, she was ambitious and driven.

It was part of what he loved about her. She complemented his more laid-back, easygoing personality perfectly. They did so many things together, and they paired well. Obviously, she hadn't shared his opinion. Or maybe she just felt like he would hold her back.

"Maybe I should go after her?" Vera said softly after Mertie disappeared into the healing garden.

Garnet didn't know what to say. He knew why she had run away. It was all him. That, and she had gotten a good look at her daughter. She had probably recognized the eyes, the features, everything that looked exactly like Mertie. But it had been his name, when he had introduced himself, that had set her off.

But he couldn't go after her. He had agreed to lead the Bible study this morning. He couldn't just abdicate his responsibilities because he wanted to go after the only woman he had ever loved.

"That might be a good idea. Or I can do it. I'm not sure what's wrong. She seemed to be looking forward to coming." Amara, Mertie's sister, spoke from where she sat on the swing beside Hobert, her fiancé.

They had asked Garnet to marry them once the church voted him in, which they seemed to think was a given. Garnet wasn't so sure, but he had agreed and liked the idea that Mertie's sister would be his first wedding.

"I'll go. Unless you have an idea of what might be wrong?" Vera spoke to Amara, glancing at Garnet. He wasn't sure if people had put two and two together and realized that she left as soon as he had mentioned his name.

His eyes shifted, and he looked over at Dabney. She didn't seem the slightest bit concerned, having sat down on the step and opened her book again. He hadn't mentioned that her mother was originally from Raspberry Ridge. He spoke about her as little as possible, other than mentioning multiple times over the years how much different Dabney was from her mother in personality. Dabney had always said she took after him, and he didn't correct her.

"I have no idea," Amara said, looking truly perplexed.

"If you don't mind going after her, Miss Vera, I would appreciate it. And we'll get started with our Bible study." Garnet decided that it would probably be best for him to step in, although Vera was very pregnant with the twins she carried. She wouldn't have offered if she didn't think she could do it. Typically people looked to the leader to make decisions. And since no one seemed to know what the trouble with Mertie might be, and he did, he figured he should take responsibility.

"I'll look for you if you're still talking to her after we're finished," he said as Vera stood. She had a hand on her belly but didn't seem to be in distress.

Vera and Dominic had someone watching the four children that they had adopted. They had gone from having no children to having four, and she and her husband couldn't look happier. She nodded at him and then stepped off the porch, walking with purpose, although not nearly as quickly as Mertie had, toward the healing garden.

Garnet watched her go for just a moment before he turned back to his Bible and said a small prayer. He hadn't come intending to upset Mertie. He hadn't expected her to be here. It was just... He wanted to say bad timing, but he knew there was no such thing. For some reason,

God wanted them here at the same time, and while Garnet had hopes as to what that might be, he also knew that it might just be for him to be able to face the past and realize that some pain never went away.

He couldn't begin to fathom what God might be wanting to teach Mertie.

Sometimes lessons were painful though, and he wished there was something he could do to mitigate that. But it would be foolishness on his part to try to protect her from what God wanted her to learn. It would make her a better person if she allowed it. And from what he knew about her, she would allow it, although she wouldn't like it.

"All right, everyone, if you would open your Bibles to the next chapter we're reading together, I'll start. I understand you typically read about five or ten verses, and then the next person begins. There are some rather difficult names in this chapter, so I hope you forgive me if I butcher them."

He said that mostly because sometimes people were a little embarrassed or self-conscious about the difficult words that they could come across in the Bible. They looked at a preacher like he somehow had some kind of superhuman ability to know how to pronounce them. That couldn't be further from the truth, and Garnet appreciated the murmur of laughter that went around the group as he spoke. It was his experience that people could relate to someone who could admit that they weren't perfect.

He had been looking forward to leading the Bible study. The people here would be the people in his congregation, the core group, the workers, the people who helped when he needed it and supported him and encouraged him and kept the little church open.

But he found his mind drifting to Mertie and what Miss Vera might be saying to her.

Four

Mertie tried to breathe, but her lungs felt like they had a hard metal band around them and refused to expand.

She sat down heavily on a bench in the healing garden, barely noticing the profusion of flowers that bloomed around her, although the soothing sound of flowing water permeated the air and made its way into her mind and heart, relaxing her just a bit.

She closed her eyes, tried to take another breath.

Garnet was here. Here. In Raspberry Ridge, and she had four weeks that she had blocked out of her schedule to be here. He was going to be the new pastor, candidating the next two weeks, leading Bible studies, doing all the things that she, as a Christian speaker and author, would be expected to attend in town.

She wanted to bury her head in her hands, cry, shake her fist at God, and ask why?

But she knew better. First of all, crying never solved anything, and although she had indulged in the luxury at various times in her life, it wasn't something that she did habitually or even naturally. Naturally, she took the bull by the horns and twisted him to do exactly what she wanted. She didn't typically sit around wringing her hands and moaning her lot in life.

Lord, why? Why now? Why...Just why?

She didn't for one second think that it might be something other than God arranging this. But she had worked to put this behind her. Worked to try to forget, to ignore the tug on her heart every time she thought of her daughter. Garnet would have taken care of her like he said he would. She thought he was going to put her up for adoption. She hadn't wanted anyone to know. Not a soul. It would ruin everything she had planned for her life, if it came out, but Garnet had promised it wouldn't.

And so far, he had kept his promise completely. She hadn't heard a whisper, although she had kept her nose to the ground constantly, always afraid that something was going to happen to blow up all the work that she had put into her career, into being a top and influential speaker and writer. It was because she wanted to lead people to Jesus. Because she wanted to encourage Christians, because she wanted Christians to be equipped for the fight that most of them didn't even know they were in. So many Christians thought being a Christian was about peace and love and joy and what they could get for themselves. They didn't stop to think about what they were supposed to be doing as a child of God, as a follower of Jesus, as someone whose sins had been forgiven. They wanted to think they were supposed to bask in all the good things and didn't have to get their hands dirty actually doing anything.

She had found it was her mission in life to preach to them otherwise. That there was no such thing as a Christian who just sat around and rested on their laurels. They were to be engaged in the fight. To shed the light of Christ abroad, so others could come to know Him, so that the world could be a better place.

She was so passionate about what she believed, and she believed with all her heart that her passion had come from the Lord.

Why, God? Why now? Why are You doing this to me? Why did You bring me face-to-face with my past, with everything I wanted to keep hidden?

She didn't suppose it was a sin to ask God why. But she also wasn't surprised when He didn't answer her.

This was where her faith should come into action. She should rest in the knowledge that God had everything under control, and her worrying about things was not going to make a difference. The only problem was, she loved the idea of building a career, of reaching as many people as possible with her message of get into the battle now, fight the good fight, don't just sit around waiting for God to give you joy and peace and love. Go out and work for Him, look at the harvest fields which were white and ready for harvest as Jesus said.

Maybe she should do more studying on faith, since she was a little embarrassed now in her panic attack. Although she was happy she didn't have to face her past right away, she knew the day was coming, the time was coming, could even be here today, and she needed to be ready. This was unexpected, but not something she couldn't handle.

"Do you mind if I sit down?"

Mertie looked up, startled. She hadn't heard Vera's approach.

"Sure." She pulled breath into her lungs, grateful that they expanded the way they were supposed to, for the most part. Her chest still felt abnormally tight. She definitely felt tense, and her mind was still feverishly going over possibilities where she could potentially leave town and never return.

She had already promised her sisters she would be here to help, and she didn't want to go back on her word. That wasn't something that a person in her position should do or something any Christian should ever do.

She tried to pull her Christian speaker and writer mantle around her like a protective cloak. She didn't want to show weakness. Weakness was bad.

But she had known Vera since she was little, and if there was a nicer person on the planet, Mertie wasn't sure where they existed or how that would be possible.

"Is everything okay?" Vera said, putting a hand over top of her hands which were clenched in her lap. She deliberately loosened her grip but did not move her hands out from underneath Vera's motherly touch.

"I guess being back here just brings back some memories."

"Hard memories?" Vera asked, although she probably didn't need to.

"Yeah. Don't we all have things we would rather forget?" She didn't want to go into the past, didn't want to admit what she had done. But at the same time, it hadn't been in front of her face like it had today. Not just Garnet, but...her daughter.

That was probably the biggest thing. She had given away a child, a baby, and had tried as hard as she could not to think about that baby again, but at times, especially when she lay in bed at night, she would wonder what happened to her, wonder who had adopted her, what her family was like, if she was being taken care of. There had been a few times where she had wished that she hadn't given her away and that she could find her, bring her back.

But then it would open that can of worms where her reputation as a Christian speaker would be in tatters.

"I suppose that in your line of work, it's fairly important that your life be crystal clear and squeaky clean. People probably look at you with a high-powered microscope, trying to find anything wrong, any reason why they could dismiss your work and call you a hypocrite."

Mertie was surprised. Vera was so astute. "You're absolutely right. I'm held to a higher standard than anyone I know."

"That has to wear on you."

"I guess I love rising to the challenge. I love trying as hard as I can to be as good as I can. I do not believe, not for one second, in works-based salvation. The only way to heaven is through the shed blood of Jesus, like the Bible says. But I want to be pure, I want to be good, I want to follow Jesus and his commands and hear him say 'well done.' You know? That's my only goal." For the most part. Every once in a while, she would look at the bottom line and have goals related to money and production, but she didn't see that as a bad thing. If she didn't aim at anything, she wasn't going to hit anything. But that wasn't what she lived for. What she breathed for. What she wanted with all her heart and soul.

"I can kind of relate to that. When I'm designing a garden, I want it to be the best that it possibly can be. Better than anything. The very best that I can do. I want it to give people hope and peace and light and love and make them feel comforted and relaxed and inspired. It's what I live and breathe when I'm designing."

"Yeah. That sounds right."

"I guess it's the same with being a mom. I have four little ones, and two more on the way, and I want more than I want my next breath to be the very best mom that I can be for them. To teach them right from wrong, and to help them to grow up to love and serve Jesus. It's what I want. It's what I live for."

"I probably would be consumed with motherhood that same way. I've often thought that I couldn't be a speaker and writer and also a mother. I can't put my heart and soul into both."

"Yeah. Some people can turn that on and off, be the very best mom at home, then walk into the office and be the very best there, but that's just not me." Vera lifted a shoulder and looked around where they were sitting.

Mertie noticed the beautiful flowers, the graceful flow of the water, the soothing nature that was around her, and she remembered reading an article about Vera, and it struck her then. "You designed this?" She lifted one hand, sliding it out from underneath Vera's motherly touch, and indicated the garden around them.

"Yes. My husband and I built it together. It…saved my marriage."

Mertie didn't say anything to that. She'd given plenty of marriage advice over the years, even though she'd never been married herself. To her way of thinking, marriage was just living Christian principles, only on a microscopic, daily basis. If you gave unconditional love, unconditional forgiveness, unconditional kindness to your spouse, and treated them the way you wanted to be treated, putting the golden rule into effect, and if your spouse did the same, there was no way your marriage could be anything but beautiful. Yes, she understood the different genders were given different jobs, but Christian principles still applied. And they had to apply regardless of what one spouse did.

"I've done some marriage counseling and some marriage instruction over the years, but since I'm not married myself, I try not to speak on it too much. People want to hear from someone with experience. Someone who's been in the trenches, so to speak, and that's not me. Not for marriage."

"You have different things to talk about." Vera left that statement rather open ended. Maybe it was an opening for Mertie to tell her what was wrong.

"I do." She wasn't going to. She couldn't tell her. She couldn't let her know that the issues she had were so big they could blow up her career, and they could ruin her daughter's life too. There were people who wanted to see Christians fail so badly that they would destroy their family and jump on any attempt to knock those Christians down. She didn't want her daughter to get hurt in any way.

She never had, but now that she'd seen her, seen how...composed and sweet and innocent she seemed, she wanted to protect her even more.

She owed Garnet a thank you. A huge thank you for raising her daughter to be such a composed young lady.

It didn't even occur to her that she might be wrong, that the girl she had seen wasn't her daughter, and that Garnet hadn't kept her.

She was racking her brain, trying to remember whether Garnet had ever promised that he would actually take her to an adoption agency like she had asked.

She couldn't remember. She had just known that she needed the "problem" taken care of, but that would not include, would never include, abortion. That idea was unthinkable. Although tempting. Very tempting, because then no one would ever know.

Still, there were some things a person just couldn't do, and killing an innocent baby was one of them for her.

Making sure that it had a better life apart from her, now that was something she felt was a sacrifice on her part, but something that she did for the benefit of her child and not the benefit of herself. Although now, it would definitely benefit her career to keep the secret.

"I don't want to push you into saying anything you don't want to say, but I know for me, sometimes it helps for me to talk about things. My husband and I went through a difficult time after the loss of our son."

"I didn't know. I'm so sorry."

Vera shook her head, looking serene and completely unbothered. She took her hand that had been lying over top of Mertie's and pointed to the crosses that were just over her shoulder.

"That's what this garden was for. For healing, after our loss. I withdrew into myself, and Dominic threw himself into his work. We drifted apart, because of the different ways we handled our grief and how we didn't handle it together. I suppose I have no idea what the proper way is for a married couple to handle the loss of their child. Maybe it's okay to need some time to yourself. Maybe it's okay to need to be busy. I just know that you can drift apart before you realize it and that it's really difficult to come back together."

"I've met some people like that. Sometimes, it seems like the wife, especially, blames the husband."

Vera nodded. "That might have been part of my problem. I wanted to take Trent to the ER, and my husband thought I was worrying too much. I don't know that his life would have been spared if I had taken him, but I do know that I delayed calling for an ambulance because my husband didn't think it was necessary."

"He was there?" Mertie said softly, knowing it would have been hard to call an ambulance when her husband was standing over her telling her not to.

"No. He was away. Working. I was scared, alone, and maybe I tried to downplay it when I talked to him so that I didn't come off as one of those helicopter moms who panic when their child sneezes."

She didn't quite laugh, but she did snort a little. She'd met mothers like that. They practically followed their children around with pillows under their behind, waiting to catch them so that nothing bad could ever happen to them.

"It's important that children suffer, they don't understand or learn how to handle it if they don't. But it's really hard to know where that line is. Where do you stop allowing them to handle things on their own and start panicking."

"Right. It was time to panic, and I should have gone ahead and done the full-blown panic, but... I didn't."

Vera looked off, staring at the flowing water, as though contemplating a long-ago time and wondering if she might have done something different whether there would have been a different outcome.

"But the thing to remember is, God is in control. He's in control whether I call immediately or whether I don't call at all. I'm not saying that God doesn't sometimes allow us to experience the consequences of our actions, but nothing happens to me that has not been approved by Him first. And that's what enabled me to not blame my husband. It wasn't his fault. It wasn't mine, either. But it took me a long time to figure that out."

"Yeah. Sometimes we know what's right, we just don't always see it immediately." Was that what was happening to her right now? God had led her here to Raspberry Ridge at the exact time that Garnet was here with their daughter, and God had arranged it, and instead of Mertie seeing that and going with it, she ran away, not wanting to face whatever it was that God wanted her to stand and face and learn.

Absolutely that was what she was doing.

"I guess I'm doing that now," she said softly, not wanting to go into the fact that she had a daughter, and that she was here in Raspberry Ridge, and as far as Mertie knew, she had no idea that Mertie was her mom. She didn't know what Garnet had told her.

"Standing and deliberately not looking at what God wants you to?" Vera asked, and Mertie nodded.

"I guess I just needed you to come and tell me that I might not want to face it, but if it's here, I have to."

Vera smiled, a maternal, kind, compassionate smile. The kind of smile that made Mertie want to put her head on her shoulder and lean into her warmth and comfort.

"You know, it hasn't been that long since you've lost your parents. It takes a while to get over loss like that. Don't be too hard on yourself."

Mertie hadn't even thought about that. She loved her parents, but they had been very involved in their business and seemed rather distant throughout their childhood. She mourned their loss, more because she mourned the loss of the family unit, but it was not like she mourned the loss of a companion or friend. Since neither of her parents seemed to be that to her. But she did want to stay close to her sisters. Or be close to her sisters, since they hadn't really been close.

"Thank you for your compassion. I suppose losing one's parents is an adjustment no matter what your relationship was."

"Sure. You have to adjust the way you see yourself in life. You're no longer tied to someone who's here, but...standing on your own, I suppose. Although, God is never moved, and He's standing right there, wanting us to turn to Him."

Mertie didn't know how many times she had told that exact same thing to someone, and yet it seemed like Christians could always use the reminder.

They sat in silence for a while, with the water flowing, the soothing sound seeming to pour strength and backbone back into Mertie. She needed to talk to Garnet. Preferably without their daughter around, so they could get things hashed out. Make sure that Garnet hadn't told their daughter anything that Mertie didn't know, and that they could decide together on exactly how much they would tell her.

"I'm going to go back, but if you need me, my door is always open. It might be a little crazy at my house, but it's always open." Vera squeezed her hand and then stood. She took one step away and then turned. "Your daughter is beautiful, just like you are."

Mertie's mouth hung open, and she didn't see Vera walk away, unable to respond to her comment. Even if she hadn't already decided it would be best to tell the world what was going on, she would have had to decide to actually do it, since there was no way she was going to be able to hide it.

Five

Mertie hadn't been at Bible study that morning. After the way she took off yesterday, Garnet knew he shouldn't have been surprised.

But a man could hope.

A man could spend his life hoping and always be disappointed.

Or he could assume that God knew what He was doing and that the life he had was the life he was supposed to have.

Looking back, he wasn't sure what decisions he could have made differently that would make things turn out the way he really wanted them to. He had to admit, God knew best. Even when it wasn't what he wanted.

"Is it okay if I take my book, go to the healing garden, and read for a bit?" Dabney stood in front of him on his parents' front porch, and it took Garnet a minute to bring his mind back to the present.

"Sure. But if you're going down to the lake, I don't want you to swim without someone with you."

They had always gone by the buddy rule. Growing up by the lake, it was intrinsic for him, but since Dabney hadn't, he hadn't drilled into her head that she never swim alone from the time she was little the way he had, so he felt like he needed to remind her.

As usual, she didn't look irritated, but just nodded her head and said, "I wasn't going to go down to the lake. But I really like the garden. I think it's the water."

She carried her book, a real, live book, and walked off the porch, walking sedately toward the garden.

He watched her go. She was getting so big. And he knew he was blessed. She had hardly ever given him a day's worth of trouble. A few scary times when she had been sick, once when she had gotten stung by a bee and he had to take her to the emergency room for some treatments and had gotten a permanent EpiPen, but other than that, she had been a dream.

He had never questioned his decision to keep her himself, rather than trying to find a couple to adopt her. Until now.

The pastoral committee had asked about her mother, and Garnet had not gone into great detail. He just said he wasn't divorced and her mother wasn't in the picture. Both true statements.

"Honey, how did Bible study go this morning?" his mother asked, coming to the door and pushing it open.

She had been the full-time caretaker for his dad for the last six months since his dad had suffered a stroke and been wheelchair-bound.

That was part of the reason Garnet had decided to come to Raspberry Ridge and apply for the pastoral position. Even though he would be taking a huge cut in salary.

"It went well. I wish you could go." His mother refused to leave her husband for that long. Typically morning and evening were the busiest times, getting him out of bed and ready for the day and then getting him ready for bed in the evening. She wouldn't go until he was up, and his normal time to get up was right in the middle of the prayer meeting.

"This just isn't my season," his mother said, coming out and sitting down in a rocking chair. Their front porch was picturesque, with several rocking chairs, a nice porch swing, and a shade tree right off to the side. There wasn't much sidewalk to speak of in Raspberry Ridge, but their house sat a little bit back away from the road, and parking was off the street. It was a perfect place for a kid to grow up, and he had an idyllic childhood.

He felt a little guilty for pulling his daughter out of her friend circle and making her move right in the middle of her teenage years. He tried to think about how unsettled that would make him feel, but he could hardly imagine. He always felt so grounded and secure as an only child growing up, his parents both in the home and no drama.

So much different than Dabney's childhood.

"Do you think they're enjoying the way you lead Bible study?" his mother asked after a few moments of silence.

"They seem to. There were almost as many people there today as there were yesterday." The only one who hadn't shown back up was Mertie. And he wasn't sure whether he could count her as yesterday's participant or not, since she had been there for the beginning but had left before he had started teaching.

"I just feel bad that you've come the whole way to Raspberry Ridge to help me out, and you might not even get that job."

"If I don't, I'll know it's because God has something else in store for me. But there's no question in my mind that I'm supposed to be here with you and Dad." He could not help but take care of his parents. Not after they'd done so much for him. He didn't really understand the idea of a child not taking care of their parents. Regardless, everyone had their own situation and he didn't want to judge. He just knew that his place was with his parents for as long as he could handle it.

"You don't need to worry about anything, Mom. I'm still getting some income from my blog and from the social media posts I do. It's going to be enough." It wouldn't be enough for him to make a house payment or car payment, it definitely wouldn't be enough for him to pay for college for Dabney, but he hadn't raised her to expect him to pay for her. His car was paid off, and as long as he lived with his parents, the only thing he had to do was buy health insurance. Which wasn't cheap, but since he didn't need anything else, he would be able to get by.

"Your blog must not take much time."

"I wrote one this morning before I went to Bible study. And I wrote it on the same thing I was teaching in Bible study, so I was kind of killing two birds with one stone." He found that when he studied something in the Bible, he tended to go deep. As deep as he could, and he always ended up with more material than he could ever use. So he figured he might as well write a blog post about it. The social media posts were short excerpts from his blog, punchy lines that were short enough to draw attention, at least that's what he hoped.

"Are you working on that book?" his mom asked, the rocking chair going, but her hands and fingers on her lap were not still.

"Mom. I promise you. You do not need to worry. God has me."

"I'm not worried," she said, looking over at him with a slight bit of irritation on her face, but her hands didn't quit moving.

"Mother," he said, lifting a brow and then looking deliberately at her lap where one hand picked at the fingernail on the other.

"You're my son. I just... I want you to be safe and happy. I figure that if you come here, you're never going to get married, and I always still hope that you would."

He allowed a few beats to pass. He didn't want to talk about it and really didn't want to be honest, but it was his mother and he'd do his best.

"I'd like to, but I'd rather not be married to anyone than married to the wrong woman."

People told him he was too picky, and maybe that was true. He wanted a woman who studied the Bible before she met him, and not just because she knew it was important to him. Of course, if she was influenced to start studying after they met, that was a different story, but he didn't want someone who was just doing it for show, who was going to quit the second they said "I do." He wanted someone whose faith was strong on her own. Someone who was so close to the Lord that he could get her advice and opinion on things, he could talk to her about the deep things he thought about, that she wouldn't think he was crazy or nuts for eschewing so many of the things that society thought were important and wanting instead a simple life, filled with trying to put biblical principles into practice.

"How's your book coming?"

"I suppose it's coming okay. I'll have more time to work on it here." If he were hired, which it looked like he would be, he could write his book around the sermons he preached. Or the opposite, preach the sermons around whatever chapter he was writing in his book.

But that really wasn't what he was thinking about.

"I heard there were some ladies who visit a local, newly married woman, giving her some advice on her marriage and her home. Vera spearheads that. If you are interested in tagging along, I'm sure they would be interested in having you."

"I'll have to make sure I talk to her about that," he said. Those were the kinds of things he wanted to do, to help people. To strengthen marriages and help people get closer to the Lord.

"Are you ever going to tell anyone about Dabney?"

Garnet felt his eyes widen and was glad he was looking away from his mother. Back when he had first gotten Dabney, he hadn't told his parents who the mother was. She had been classified as an abandoned baby, and he had been able to adopt her, although there had been a lot of hoops and red tape. But he had been able to do it without disclosing the identity of her mom. There were only two people in the entire world, as far as he knew, who knew about Dabney. Himself and Mrs. Calvin.

He had never questioned Mertie about how she had been able to hide her pregnancy and, even more, how she'd been able to hide the birth. Those were secrets that Mertie still carried.

"I suppose coming back here, a lot of people are going to wonder."

"Including your mother."

"I'm sorry, Mom. There are some things I just can't talk about. And unfortunately, that is one of those things."

"Don't you think Dabney has the right to know the truth?"

"I think she does." He needed to talk to Mertie. Dabney definitely should know the truth. But he wasn't the one who was at liberty to tell it. It was Mertie. And obviously she didn't want to face it since she had gone running out of Bible study yesterday. He'd been praying about it since, hoping that she would come to her senses and realize that perhaps she would be set free by telling the truth.

"But?" his mother prompted when he didn't say anything more.

"But it's not my truth to tell." He shifted, moving over toward the steps. "Dabney went to the healing garden to read a book. As long as you think everything will be okay with Dad, I'm going to walk to the church and work on Sunday's sermon." He didn't add that he was going to pray about the situation. He felt like it could be better handled in a different way, but he also felt like his hands were tied, and it wasn't up to him to handle it. It was up to Mertie.

"All right. I can call you if I need you," his mom said, sounding resigned but not angry. Of course she was going to be upset. But she respected the fact that he couldn't tell other people's secrets. That some things just weren't the way they wanted them to be, and that had to be okay.

He grabbed the bag with his laptop, notebooks, and Bible in it and walked off the porch, giving his mom a smile as he did so. And then he walked up the street toward the alleyway where the little white church sat up on a hill, with a beautiful view of the lake in the distance, and overlooking the town as well. The cemetery up there was beautiful, with Vera and Dominic Miller taking over the care of it and making the entire spot peaceful and beautiful.

As he walked, he enjoyed the scenery, but he was also praying. Praying that there would be a resolution to this that would not hurt Dabney, that would not ruin Mertie's career. He could be wrong, but he bet that was what the issue was.

Regardless, it couldn't be the only thing he thought about. He had to focus on the sermon he was going to give on Sunday, the one the next Sunday, and doing what he could to further God's kingdom here, whether he became the pastor in Raspberry Ridge or not.

Six

"We have an entire month to do this, you don't have to get everything finished in one day."

Mertie ignored her sister and continued to scrub the deck chairs.

"Mertie," Amara said, her tone demanding Mertie's attention.

Mertie didn't want to stop. She didn't want to give herself any time to think. And the sooner they got the stuff done, the sooner she could leave and never come back.

Amara's hand landed on her forearm, forcing her to stop scrubbing and to look her sister in the eye.

"What is going on with you?" Amara said, exasperation in her voice, but caring and compassion there as well. Her sister loved her and wanted the best for her. Even if they weren't as close as they could be, Mertie didn't doubt that. And as the oldest and the one with the commanding personality who organized and led naturally, it was her fault they weren't close.

"Nothing. I just don't see any point in sitting around twiddling our thumbs when there's work to do." That wasn't entirely true, but she wasn't the kind of person who sat around and waited for somebody else to take care of things. She did it herself.

"You don't need to work yourself into the ground. I'm going to go out on the boat with Hobert late tonight, and I wanted to make sure you knew that. I don't want you feeling like you have to work when I'm not here."

"Somebody needs to do it," she said, not meaning to sound nasty. But she was a little frustrated with her middle sister, Olive, who hadn't shown up at all.

"It's not Olive's fault she's gotten stuck in South America and can't get a flight out."

There'd been something about quarantine and then an issue with her passport, and through it all, Olive had not managed to make it home. Although Mertie wondered just how much of that was because she really didn't want to come home.

She had preached just as loud and long as she could about not making assumptions about other people and always assuming the best. She reminded herself that she needed to live what she had been preaching all this time.

She had just opened her mouth to tell her sister not to worry about her, when her phone rang.

Mertie almost didn't answer it. She was supposed to be on vacation, and her personal assistant had strict orders not to bother her unless it was urgent.

All of her other calls were forwarded to an automatic voice message. Then her personal assistant could go through them at her leisure, responding to the ones that couldn't wait until Mertie was back in.

She had never actually taken off this much time before, but it was imperative that she get the house cleaned and sold so she could focus on her career.

There was a part of her that also wanted to develop relationships with her sisters. She could hardly do that if she was running back and forth trying to keep her business afloat.

"You can go ahead and get that. I'm going back in to wash the windows." With that, Amara disappeared back inside the house, and Mertie pulled her phone out of her pocket, seeing her assistant's number before she swiped and said, "Hello?"

She almost added that she had asked not to be interrupted unless it was extremely urgent, but typically Sandy, her assistant, was quite good and completely dependable.

"I've been screening all your emails, and there are a few you might want to take a look at, but when this came in today, I knew I had to reach you."

"Okay," Mertie said, suddenly all business. She had no idea what might have Sandy so excited.

"Zebedee Clinger called."

That was interesting.

"All right," she prompted when Sandy didn't say anything else. Sandy knew she had a tendency to go into unemotional, analytical mode when the stakes were high. Her reaction shouldn't be surprising. Even though the news was unexpected and extremely exciting.

"He wants to partner with you."

"Partner?" Mertie didn't typically parrot whatever Sandy said, but she didn't understand. Zebedee Clinger was the top Christian author and speaker in the United States at that moment. He didn't need a partner.

"Yes. Partner. You know his wife recently divorced him, and he feels like he's having trouble reaching women. He told me that he feels like he needs to add a woman to his team, and he wanted that woman to be you. He told me he wasn't looking at anyone else."

That was huge. That was bigger than huge. That was...career changing.

"You're right. This is definitely something I wanted to know. Thank you for calling me."

"I have an email ready. I'm going to send it to you with all of the details, everything we spoke about on the phone. He is supposed to be following up with an email as well, and then once you get that, you have everything you need in order to figure out how you're going to move forward."

It wasn't if, it was how.

The thought gave Mertie a little bit of pause, because she had just been thinking that God had brought her here to possibly change her life and her career trajectory. But... God wouldn't have thrown an opportunity like this into her lap if He hadn't wanted her to seize it and run with it. Think of all the people she could influence. Think of all the good she could do. The revival that might come to America as men and women were both being reached on a major scale for the Lord.

They spoke for a little bit longer before hanging up, with Mertie trying not to jump with excitement. It wouldn't be the thing for a well-respected Christian speaker to have a happy dance in the middle of her porch.

"Good news?" Amara said, making her startle, and her hand went to her chest.

"I didn't hear you."

"I'm sorry," Amara said, tilting her head as though waiting for Mertie to answer the question.

"Yes. Very good news. It could be a game changer for my career." She hadn't been expecting anything like that today. She had been rather preoccupied about all the other things that had been going on, and just when she was down, the Lord had sent her the very best news she could possibly have.

But there was a little nagging voice in the back of her head that asked whether the news was good, or whether it was a choice that she needed to make, to resist the temptation of power and prestige and choose instead family and the thing that looked like it would be less but could actually end up being more. More in someone's life beyond her own.

She could change a million lives, possibly more, if she accepted the opportunity that Zebedee Clinger was potentially offering.

"You look excited. Happy even. You haven't looked like that since you got here," Amara said, and Mertie knew she wasn't trying to hurt her or complain. She was just making an honest observation.

Maybe it was thinking about her daughter or about Garnet, or maybe it was the idea that being bigger meant being better. She couldn't afford to have anything wrong with her life; Christians could be merciless in their demanding that any leader they had be absolutely perfect. After all, wasn't it hypocritical to preach about something that you didn't have right in your own life?

She certainly didn't want to listen to Christian speakers who didn't have it all together.

No one else did either. So she had to make sure that every I was dotted, every T crossed, and this was not a good time for an unknown daughter to come out of the woodwork. Especially considering how she was conceived.

"I'm sorry. I am happy to be here. And I really hope that it will lead to a better relationship between you and Olive and me. I guess I've just been...preoccupied."

Seeing one's daughter for the first time since she was a baby would do that to a person.

"You know if there's something you want to talk about, I'm willing to listen."

Vera had said the same thing.

"Thank you. I'll keep that in mind."

"Great. I was coming out to let you know that I had put some hamburger in the refrigerator to thaw, in case you wanted to make something. But I'm going out on the boat tonight, and I won't be back until tomorrow."

"Hobert is fishing at night?" she asked, knowing that her sister could make whatever decision she wanted to, but it kind of sounded like they were spending the night together on the boat.

"Yeah. Actually, he was telling me that sometimes fish bite better at night under a full moon. That's what we have tonight. So we're going to try it. Honestly, we're fishing." She gave Mertie a smile, a friendly one, with no rancor in it, so Mertie didn't feel like Amara had taken offense over her question. After all, if someone was trying to help you do right, it shouldn't offend you when they asked you a question.

Unless you didn't like being pulled away from the brink of sin. There were times in Mertie's life where she hadn't appreciated someone's effort to help her do right. Maybe now was one of those times. She could have talked to Amara or Vera, but the main reason she didn't want to was because she figured that they would encourage her to get to know her daughter.

Mertie wasn't sure she could handle that. There were some deep emotions involved, hard feelings, and things that she had known from the beginning that she would probably want to keep buried for the rest of her life. She hadn't expected to come face-to-face with her daughter later. Now, the desire to know her, to see what kind of woman she was becoming, to...see if she needed a mom...

She didn't even know if Garnet was married. Maybe he was.

She hadn't seen a wife on the porch, but that didn't mean there wasn't one.

She worked for another hour, but her head was far, far away. She was so torn about what decision she should make, she packed her things up early, deciding that it might be helpful to go down to the healing garden and just sit and listen to the water, and ask the Lord to show her clearly what she was supposed to do.

She already knew what she wanted to do, and she already knew what would help the most people. Obviously, accepting Zebedee Clinger's offer.

That was even more clear to her when she checked her emails and saw that the promised one from him was there.

She read through it quickly, then read it one more time.

He was offering a full partnership, speaking engagements, a three-book deal, cowritten together, almost guaranteed to sell millions of copies, and a speaking tour starting the next summer.

Not only would she be touching millions of lives, literally, but she would be making enough money that she would never have to worry about money again.

She could donate to whatever she wanted to donate to, help with child trafficking, rescue babies whose parents didn't want them.

There was so much good she could do, it was almost a no-brainer to write back immediately and say that she accepted his offer and his people could talk to her people and they could hash out a contract between them.

But something held her back. Kept her from replying to the email. That prompted her to carefully put her things away, cleaning up her mess, taking one last look at the outside of the house which was half scrubbed, but still needed a good bit of work, and then turn her face to town, grabbing her pen and notebook and her Bible as well.

Seven

"You have to make sure the chicken is all cut up into small pieces, then you add this," Garnet said, talking to Dabney, who hung on his every word. She had shown interest in cooking and keeping house in the week or so since they had moved to Raspberry Ridge. Maybe it was because of the change in her life she needed to have some kind of grounding. Or maybe it was just her age. He wasn't sure, but he was more than happy to work with her in the kitchen. Spending time with his daughter was his favorite activity.

"If I'd known you guys were going to take over the cooking, I would have asked you to move in years ago." His mother spoke as she walked into the kitchen. Garnet had felt a little guilty since his dad had not had a very good morning. Helen had shooed him away when Dabney had asked if they were going to cook lunch together. He hadn't wanted to leave his mom, but he supposed that she was used to her husband's sour moods.

Garnet couldn't imagine how frustrating it must be to not be able to do everything that he used to do. His dad had always been someone who enjoyed tinkering with things, who always had a project going on, or several projects. Now, he couldn't even get out of bed without help.

If nothing else, moving to Raspberry Ridge had given him more of a burden to pray for his parents. His mom, who must be eligible for sainthood with the way she had cared for her husband, had shown him the meaning of grace and love as she worked on navigating this new reality, making him realize anew that living a life that glorified God was more important than getting and doing what he wanted.

Garnet wasn't sure how he would react if he had a stroke and couldn't move.

At least his dad had a wife who could take care of him. Garnet didn't have that, although he supposed Dabney would do it. But he didn't want her to have to care for her father. Surely she had other things she wanted to do with her life, although again, the older he got, the more he realized that it was less about what a person wanted to do and more about facing what God had given them and doing it with grace and love and kindness.

His mother grabbed a glass of water and exited the kitchen.

Garnet reached for the stove, with his mouth open to tell Dabney what to do in the next step of the rotisserie chicken with stuffing casserole they were making, when Dabney spoke.

"That woman, the one who ran away from the prayer meeting?"

Garnet froze, his hand reaching for the stove, his mouth open. He had thought that Dabney was reading and wasn't paying attention.

"Yeah?" To his surprise, his voice came out as casually as he intended it to.

"She hasn't been back."

"No. She hasn't."

"You think you should go visit her?" Dabney's innocent question, prompted by her love for her fellow human, even a stranger, and a desire to see everyone come to know Christ, should have made him happy, but instead it sent tendrils of fear down his spine, chilling him to the bone.

"Probably." He didn't know what else to say. How could he tell her, "She's your mother, and I wanted to stay as far away from her as I could, because I'm pretty sure she doesn't want to have anything to do with us."

He kind of understood Mertie's position, and he definitely couldn't argue with her. He would never be in that position. Never know how that felt. Never know what it felt like to give birth to a child and to love the being that came out of her body more than life itself. Although it was hard for him to imagine loving anyone more than he loved Dabney.

On top of all of that mess, there was the friendship that they had shared for more than a decade growing up. The things they had done together, memories and activities that floated through his mind sometimes, especially in the evenings after a long, hard day when he would sit on the porch in Raspberry Ridge and it felt exactly the same way it had twenty years ago when he'd been growing up, running around with Mertie, swimming and laughing and feeling free, without the pressure of adult life. They were precious memories, and then of course, over the years, he gradually realized that not only did he like her as a friend, but there was a deep attraction, at least on his part, that made him want to be more.

It had only taken him seeing her one time to realize that that attraction had not gone away. Not for him. But she didn't see him like that, she was too businesslike, too driven, too determined to wrestle life and make it be what suited her.

"Maybe we should do that today," Dabney said as he gathered himself and finished turning on the oven before he turned away to grab the next ingredient.

"This might be one I need to do myself."

"Why? Are you afraid she's going to curse me because she hates God, and you're afraid that I'll see that she hates God and decide I hate God too?"

Sometimes his daughter was too astute, and sometimes she totally missed the mark. This was one of the latter. Which he was grateful for, because he didn't want her to know the truth.

"Well, I definitely don't want that to happen to you. But God gives everyone free choice, and you're free to choose to love the Lord and serve Him or to do something else with your life."

"Sometimes I feel like I really want to, and then sometimes I feel like that's going to be too hard. And God isn't going to let me do what I want to do. He's probably going to send me to Africa to be a missionary there or something."

"I suppose that's the first thing about being a Christian, you turn from what you were doing, it's called repentance, and you offer your life to Jesus. It doesn't mean that it no longer matters what you want, what you like, how you feel. That you'll do what's right and what God wants you to. Sometimes that means you go directly against your feelings."

A little bit the way he had, when he had walked away from his attraction to Mertie and raised Dabney. Of course, it had taken him all of about three seconds to fall in love with Dabney, but it had been extremely difficult to give up his hopes that he and Mertie would end up together.

"Sometimes, if I'm honest, it feels like following God just means a life of getting nothing that I want. That's not the slightest bit appealing to a teenager. I don't want to present following God to you that way. Because He knows best. He knows what's going to make us content, even more than we do ourselves. But more than that, He knows what's going to grow us into better people."

And that was absolutely the truth. Everything that had happened had caused him to grow up and become a better man. Even if he hadn't gotten the thing that he wanted the most.

They had the casserole in the oven and were cleaning up the kitchen when his mom came in again. She collapsed in a chair and stretched her feet out in front of her.

"That was a rough morning," she said, pushing some of her hair back away from her face. "I wonder if anyone around here would be interested in making some cookies. Cookies usually make a rough morning better."

"I'll make cookies! Dad taught me how to make chocolate chip. But I'd really like to know how to make snickerdoodles. Those are my favorite."

"Really?" his mom said, her smile brightening. Seeing that smile, seeing her interact with Dabney, made Garnet feel that coming back home was the smartest decision he could make and exactly what God wanted him to do, even though it seemed counterintuitive, since he'd left a well-paying job and was candidating for a church that couldn't even afford to pay him a full-time wage.

"I just so happen to be an expert at making snickerdoodle cookies, and I can show you all of my secrets."

His mother put her hand on the table and pushed back away from the chair, standing up and walking over to Dabney, who put her arms around her grandmother. The sight tore at his heart. He loved watching it, but he also thought that perhaps Dabney was starved for a woman's attention. She had to wish she had a mother. A child was hardwired to want and need both mother and father.

"Sounds like you guys are going to be busy. Can you make sure that the casserole gets taken out of the oven in time?" He waited until his mom looked up and nodded. "I think I'm going to go to the healing garden and do a little studying."

If he was going to be a pastor, he was going to have to do a lot of studying. He had what felt like endless ideas for sermons, but doing one every single week was probably quite difficult. It was like writing an hour-long speech every week.

"You go on right ahead. Dabney and I have some cookies to make."

He smiled once more at his mother and his daughter before he went out to the living room to grab his Bible from the chair where he usually sat in the morning doing his devotions. In the summer, like now, he was often outside on the front porch while he did them. And sometimes he even walked down to the healing garden, although he didn't want to be interrupted by other people who might have the same idea.

But when he came home from the townwide morning Bible study, he put his Bible back at his spot by his chair.

But now, even though he loved that spot, getting out of the house almost felt imperative in order for him to make any strides in studying.

The church had an upstairs that was entirely open and a downstairs that was entirely open, other than the bathrooms and one small closet. Even the kitchen was just basically counters on one side along with an oven and a refrigerator.

There really wasn't any place that was private for him, unless he took over the closet, which, when he peeked in, was overflowing with decades of the different things a church used throughout the seasons. Advent wreath, choir robes, old hymn books, and he even thought he saw a few puppets, along with what he assumed were bags of decorations and old Sunday school materials. He figured church women were probably among the worst hoarders in the country. If there was one page of a Sunday school booklet that hadn't been used, there was no way any good church lady he knew was going to be throwing that booklet away.

He smiled a little to himself as he stepped out of his house. Times were changing. People didn't even have Sunday school booklets anymore, and certainly the ladies of the current day were much different than the ladies of fifty or a hundred years ago.

Regardless of how different they were, he didn't think any of them would be able to solve his problems. Or even give him advice. He really had no idea what to do.

Lord, You know the solutions to my problems, and I know You're working things for my good and Your glory. I just need to have faith that You're going to work things out.

Eight

Mertie opened the healing garden's gate and pushed in. Vera had outdone herself with the design. A riot of colors greeted her, flowers blooming in profusion, and the sound of water drew her in, along the winding, paver-lined pathway.

It truly felt like an oasis, a vacation from her life, a place of comfort and rest. One of great beauty. Everywhere her eyes landed, they feasted on color and beauty.

She wandered along the path, coming to a soft waterfall where there was a small seat and a display of crosses. The sound of water felt soothing the whole way down to her soul.

It was a place that just invited a person to sit down and think about God and His goodness toward them.

She could definitely see why this was called a healing garden. It was almost as though she could feel her soul sigh with contentment and her whole being relax, allowing her mind to drift to God and His great love for her.

Somehow, sitting there, her thoughts felt more clear, her emotions less sharp, compassion and kindness stirring inside of her.

One great truth stood out among all of her other thoughts: she wanted to know Dabney. She had always wanted to know her daughter, giving her up had ripped a hole in the deepest part of her that had never healed.

Lord, is this why I'm here? You brought Garnet here and my daughter as well, and I've been running. Not just from them the other day at Bible study, but all of my life.

She was in the process of trying to figure out what she should do about her career. How she would reconcile the fact that she had a daughter, which would take the world in which she revolved by storm. It would be shocking. There would be people who would say that she wasn't fit to be in the position that she was in because of her past. Christians were notoriously unforgiving and judgmental. Of course, at times it was necessary to not have people who thought it was okay to continue in sin while they were in leadership positions, but for someone who was remorseful, who had confessed their sins and asked forgiveness for it, should they be continually punished for it?

It was often a question she had to deal with, although not for herself. And while she could easily see the difference—someone who was living in sin, willfully going against the clear commands of the Bible, was completely different than someone who had made a mistake and had turned from that sin, admitting that it was sin, and had no intention of going back to it.

But would anyone want to listen to someone like her, someone who had such a massive mistake in their past? She would lose credibility. She would lose followers, and she wouldn't be nearly as valuable a commodity to Zebedee, because while she figured that part of his offer was because he admired her and appreciated her writings, she didn't delude herself into thinking that the money and popularity she would bring to the table wasn't part of why he had asked her.

"Do you mind if I sit down?"

The question startled her so much she actually started to get up from the seat, turning toward the voice with her hand going to her throat.

The voice was different, deeper, more mature than what she remembered. But the kindness in his eyes was the same. It was Garnet. She almost didn't need to look to know.

She rose, maybe because sitting while he stood made her feel like she was at a disadvantage, but she needed this meeting, this, hopefully not confrontation, but a discussion with him.

I guess since I didn't go search for it myself, Lord, You brought it to me.

She smiled at the thought even as she held out her hand.

"Garnet. It's been a long time."

He eyed her hand, and maybe there was a bit of hurt in his eyes. At one point, they would have casually embraced, bumped shoulders, and grinned at each other. They had been best friends, after all. And had known each other better than anyone else in the world. That was before.

Finally he lifted his hand, sliding it into hers, gripping and shaking.

She wasn't sure why that made her breath catch in her throat and why she had to keep her eyes from widening and work to not stare at where their hands were clasped between them.

Their hands remained clasped between them as they slowly stopped shaking.

For the life of her, Mertie couldn't think of anything to say. Which was odd considering how many different situations she'd been in, how many different people she'd spoken with, how many people had brought their problems and questions to her, and she had calmly and rationally listened and answered. And now, her entire mind was blank, her mouth dry, with no words, no ideas forming in her head. All she could do was stare into the eyes of the man who used to be her best friend, who knew her deepest, darkest secret, at least part of it, and who had kept it faithfully all these years.

He hadn't judged her, hadn't told her what a terrible person she was, hadn't given her any grief at all, hadn't even tried to contact her.

She hadn't realized until that very moment how much she owed him.

"You've changed so much," he said, still staring at her, still gently holding her hand cradled in his.

His words snapped her out of whatever daze she'd been in, and she practically yanked her hand back away from his, jerking her eyes away and turning toward the water, wrapping her arms around her waist as though in protection.

"I'm still the same girl," she said softly, knowing that if he had said you haven't changed much, she would have argued with him about that, too. She just didn't want to agree with him right now. Which was crazy. Because she needed to talk.

As she stared at the water, words came out of her mouth. "Do you have a few minutes?"

"I have as much time as you want."

She shivered. Of course, Garnet had always been like that. Whatever she needed, he would be there to help her. He would give her whatever he could, as much as he could, anything she needed, up to and including raising her child. Although that was not what she had asked. She supposed that was just one more thing they needed to talk about.

"You can sit down." It wasn't a command, but it was a strongly worded suggestion. She always thought better on her feet. She would pace, move back and forth, the movement of her body allowing her to think. But she needed him to...be beneath her? She hated that thought, but she supposed being on her feet while he sat gave her an advantage.

He didn't argue. He took two steps to the bench, sat, setting the book and notebook that he'd been carrying on it along with his pen, stretched his legs out before him, and fixed her with his serious, intelligent gaze. Compassion oozed out of every pore, but there was something else, something elemental and manly that made it so that it was hard for her to take her eyes off him.

She took a deep breath, wondering if she should offer to allow him to go first. After all, he was the one who had found her.

"Did you know I was here?" she asked, turning to him with the idea that maybe he had deliberately come here because he wanted to talk to her. Maybe this wasn't about her leading up the conversation.

"Here in Raspberry Ridge? Yes. I recognized you immediately. You've changed."

The second time he told her she'd changed. She wasn't getting the impression that he thought the changes were good. The idea that she even wanted to ask probably showed exactly how flabbergasted he had her. Other people's opinions of her hadn't mattered for a really long time. As a Christian writer and speaker, she had to be concerned, solely and absolutely, with what God thought. Not with man. Yet here she was, wondering why he thought her changes were bad. If the vibe she was getting was accurate.

"No, here." She spread her arm around, indicating the healing garden.

"No. I came here to study for Sunday's sermon. There's no office in the church, just a big open area in the sanctuary, a big open area for the basement and fellowship hall below. It's as private as it is here." He blew out a little puff of air.

She jerked her head, then figured she might as well ask. "Where would you like to start?"

"Our conversation?" he asked immediately, his brows going up, as though he wasn't quite on her wavelength.

Before, when they'd been friends, they could finish each other's sentences, and even if they didn't think the same, he knew her well enough to know exactly what she was thinking. She had known him the same way. It was part of the draw for her.

He wasn't the same as her. She knew he would be thinking something else, something deeper, something she hadn't seen. And while they hadn't talked about it a lot, since they were just children, and in their early teens, he appreciated the same about her. They were opposites, and pretty much in every area, but through circumstance, being the only children their age in the entire town of Raspberry Ridge, they'd grown close and had learned to appreciate their differences. Even exploit them at times. They balanced each other perfectly. She shook those thoughts away.

"Yes. Our conversation. Would you like to start?"

"You're the one who said you wanted to talk to me." He didn't say he didn't have anything to say, he just pointed out that the reason he had sat down on the bench was because she invited him to do so, and she said she wanted to talk.

She couldn't be cold and aloof. Not when the first thing that she wanted to know came to her lips.

"How is she?" There was so much emotion in that one question. The despair and loneliness of the past, the absolute heartbreak of giving her daughter away. Memories of what she had done, and the knowledge that she could see in Garnet.

"She's perfect." His words were simple, spoken with absolute truth on his face and in his eyes. After he said it, a little smile turned the corners of his mouth. "Absolutely perfect."

"You love her."

He nodded. "I've loved her since the moment you set her little car seat down, her perfect face completely relaxed in trusting sleep."

"You said she looked like a monkey." Mertie almost laughed at the memory. She totally forgot until just now.

"She did. But a cute monkey. So sweet. Just precious. It hasn't changed."

"She's bigger."

"She's still just as sweet, just as precious, just as dear to me as she was the first moment I saw her." He was so sincere, so obviously in love with his daughter that Mertie was jealous.

Which was crazy. She didn't come here to strike up a romance with the man who used to be her best friend. She had no time for romance in her life when she was going to be Zebedee Clinger's partner, building an entirely new empire from their combined forces.

Mertie turned from Garnet and looked out over the top of the garden, to the deep blue of Lake Michigan. It was so beautiful here, so peaceful. Just taking a deep breath and allowing the serenity of her surroundings to calm her anxious heart.

Everything would work out. Of that, she was sure. She just wasn't sure of where her place was supposed to be or what God had in store for her. She liked it when His leading was clear, not when she had to cling to His hand in faith that He was going to show her the way whenever it was time for her to make a move.

Right now, everything inside of her was telling her that she needed to walk away, to let her sisters bear the burden of cleaning up their parents' home in order to sell it, and she needed to get out of Dixie, or she might end up blowing up everything that she had worked for for the last fifteen years.

"Does she know about me?" she asked, still staring out over the softly rippling surface of the Great Lake.

"No. I never told her anything. You asked me not to tell anyone. And I didn't. Not a soul."

"Even your parents?"

"My parents don't know. Dabney doesn't know."

"You named her Dabney?"

"It was your middle name."

She couldn't believe he remembered. Of course, it was a hard name to forget once a person knew it. It was her mother's mother's name, and when she had been younger, she had hated it, but now she appreciated the fact that she carried something of her heritage with her. Her daughter did too, thanks to Garnet.

"I can't believe you remembered," she finally murmured.

"Of course I remember." He said that like there was no doubt, but how could she know?

"I asked you to do a really hard thing."

"I would have done something a thousand times harder."

The words were simple but profound. They stirred her to her very soul.

Nine

Mertie turned to Garnet, her eyes narrow, trying to figure out what he was saying.

"Why?" Before she had come back with a baby, they had been separated for five years, while she had lived in Chicago, and he had finished going to school at Blueberry Beach, where the Raspberry Ridge kids had been bussed. He had told her that he was planning on going to school online as much as he could and commuting for the rest. Back then, it hadn't been nearly as common as it was now, but he had found a way, not wanting to leave his parents.

But she had interrupted all of those plans, and he had ended up leaving Raspberry Ridge, leaving everything because of taking her baby. Now he was saying that he would have done that and more.

While she waited, it was his turn to look away. A muscle in his jaw worked as he seemed to study the flowing water behind her.

Finally his eyes looked at her again. "I guess because of our friendship."

They had been best friends. But had their bond been that strong?

"Did you ever ask yourself whether or not I would have done the same thing for you if you had come to me and asked the same thing of me?"

"I know you would have." His words were simple, easy, and they spoke of a faith in her, in her actions, in her general goodness, that she didn't even have in herself. Not now, and certainly not fifteen years ago. She had been a spoiled, immature, young girl with a tendency toward wickedness and evil.

"How can you believe in me like that?" The words were out of her mouth before she could stop them.

"You believed in me the same way."

"You were different. We laughed about how different we were."

"About how well we fit together, about how we made each other better. About how together we could do things that apart we couldn't. Isn't this just the same?"

She tried to process his words, trying to see if she agreed, but she didn't think she could. "It wasn't a simple request. I asked you to change your life. Just like that."

"Yeah."

She'd actually asked him to find someone who would adopt her baby. She hadn't come thinking that it was going to be him taking care of her daughter. She had wanted him to take care of the details, so no one could trace the baby back to her.

"I just asked you to take care of her. See to her until she was adopted."

"That's what I did."

"You. You adopted her."

"Yes. A sealed adoption."

She hadn't known. He had taken care of everything, and she had done what he said, trusting him implicitly while working on cleaning up the mess she made of her life.

"You never told me about the father." He spoke softly, his eyes meeting hers before they went down, resting on his hands, which were clasped between his legs with his forearms resting in his lap.

"I was ashamed."

Maybe it was his posture, the humbleness he showed, the way she knew that he cared about her and loved her daughter as deeply as a human being could. Or maybe it was just because she truly was ashamed, but she took two steps over and sat down on the other end of the bench. There was plenty of room between them, but her back slumped, and her eyes were cast down.

It didn't even occur to her to look both ways to make sure no one else was listening before she started to speak. "I knew exactly what I wanted to do. I was at a Christian college, working toward becoming a Christian speaker and author. I was hoping to get a degree in journalism or something close, so I could work for someone who was doing what I wanted to do and eventually either work my way up or strike out on my own."

College hadn't been what she thought it was going to be.

"When I went to a Christian college, I thought I would be surrounded by Christians. But I was surrounded by people who said they were Christians. There's a difference."

"I know." He nodded his head once, jerking his chin down, but she had no doubt that he knew exactly what she meant. People who said that they believed in Jesus but who had never repented. Never turned from their sins, never asked for forgiveness, who just kind of picked up Jesus like a person might pick up a suitcase as they were walking along with their life, never changing.

"A person can't have Jesus and not have a changed life."

"I know. But at the time, I just saw these Christians, quote unquote, doing all these things that I had always thought were wrong and seeming to have no remorse for them."

"I think that might be the most dangerous kind of people. People who think they received salvation, think they know Jesus, but have absolutely never shown a day of repentance, and have no concept of His holiness or the power He has to change a life."

"Satan masquerades as an angel of light." She'd seen that a lot in her ministry. People being deceived.

"He sure does. He deceives us in a lot of different ways."

"I was definitely deceived. I said no the first few times my new friends asked me to go out with them, but college was harder than I thought it was going to be, and after midterms, where I got the very first F I'd ever gotten in my life, I agreed to go out. I... I was thinking of quitting."

"That's not you at all. You're not a quitter."

He knew her. She didn't quit, no matter how hard it got. That reminded her of the day they climbed the bluffs together. She couldn't remember whose idea it was, but he had gotten about four feet up and decided it was too dangerous, and he would rather be alive and live the rest of his life having never scaled the bluffs than get halfway up, lose his grip, and have his parents planning his funeral.

He had been wise.

She refused to quit.

"Remember the time you made it to the top of the bluffs?"

"I remember you standing below me, and I knew that if I fell, you would be there to catch me or die with me."

"You would have smashed me when you hit me."

"I know. I was so selfish. But as soon as you saw that I had almost made it to the top, you ran around and were there to offer me your hand as I came up over the edge."

"You wouldn't quit. I had never realized until that day that you truly wouldn't quit."

"I was stupid. Why didn't you tell me how stupid I was?"

"I think I might have."

She laughed. "I was just too stupid to listen. To actually hear what you were saying. But you were scared."

"I was. Sometimes fear keeps us from doing stupid things."

"I was scared, but my no-quit personality pushed me to the top. What's wrong with me?"

"I think you channeled that part of your personality into the right areas. It helped you become successful."

She'd become successful in the world's eyes, true. But she'd given up her daughter in the process.

"So you went out with your friends?" he asked, going back to the subject they were talking about, but leaving the question open-ended so she could fill in the details she wanted to.

"It was a one-night stand. Everyone was doing it. There was no closeness, no knowing him at all. It was something you did with whoever you spent the evening with. It wasn't even considered a walk of shame anymore whenever you woke up in some stranger's bed, sober but hungover, and gathered your things up, maybe even took a shower in his room, before you ate breakfast together, or maybe not, depending on how you felt, I suppose, and then back to your life with no strings attached."

"This is honestly not even a little appealing to me."

"It's not. It's like we've become like animals. As humans, we have the ability to think and be better, but a cow will hook up with any bull available. Spend her heat cycle with whatever bull is in the pasture with absolutely no concern for him when she's done with him, nor him for her. Then he moves on to a different cow and the cycle repeats. For animals, that's totally natural. But as a human, I don't really want to be on the level of an animal. We think we're so sophisticated, getting rid of our 'puritanical' views and being sexually liberated, but in reality, we've lowered ourselves and become animals. It makes me sick to think about it."

"I'm sorry."

"No. Maybe I needed that experience, to see how terrible it was. To see how we are degrading ourselves, when we actually think that we're so suave and debonair."

She had met people over and over again who thought the idea of being with just one person was so provincial, and it never entered their minds that rather than being elevated in their thinking, they'd actually become more base and animalistic. It never ceased to amaze her how people could be so blind. How she could be so blind.

"That's the only time I ever did something like that. I couldn't even tell you the guy's name. I honestly don't know. I saw him a few more times on campus, but either he flunked out or he was a senior. I don't even know what we talked about, but we didn't talk about anything that would help me find him. I couldn't if I wanted to for Dabney."

"Don't be so hard on yourself."

"No. I really haven't done well by her, and I suppose maybe that's why the Lord has me here. Because I didn't realize that until just now."

"We've all made mistakes."

"You haven't."

"I sure have. And I might be making a big one now. I quit my job two weeks ago. Last Friday was my last day. I applied to be pastor of the church here in Raspberry Ridge, and it doesn't even pay a full-time wage. I have nothing else lined up, other than the little bit of money I make on my socials and blog. It's not much."

He looked sheepish, and it hit her that she wasn't the only one with problems. His were just different.

"Then you have plenty of time to focus on your blog and your socials and get them to start making more money. In the meantime, if you're living with your parents, you shouldn't have a house payment—"

He put a hand up. "You're right, but we're not here to solve my problems. You were talking."

She closed her mouth immediately. There she went, trying to tell him what to do, running his issues over in her head and coming up with solutions for him, while shoving her own problems aside.

But Garnet would not allow her to. He never had.

"Sorry," she said, looking back down at her hands folded in her lap.

"Maybe you haven't changed as much as I thought you had," he said, and she heard humor in his voice.

She sighed and gave him a little smile. Unable to continue to sit still, she stood back up.

"So, you found out you were pregnant...then what?"

"That's it. I found out I was pregnant. It shocked me to pieces, and I was a little angry at God for a while. I mess up once, and I get caught. It was frustrating when I saw other "Christians" around me who were sleeping around and doing what they wanted, while their ministries flourished and the professors loved them. Anyway, I started wearing big, baggy clothes. I was able to hide my pregnancy through the end of the next semester, and then, not many people knew that I came up here and stayed with Pastor and Mrs. Calvin that summer. They helped me hide it."

"I wondered why I heard you were up here, but I barely saw you that summer. I felt like there was this huge chasm between us and I couldn't cross it."

"I'm sorry. It was all my fault. Mrs. Calvin got me a job online, which, back then, was rather rare. But I was able to work for several pastors out in the Midwest who wanted their sermons organized into a book. I spent the summer doing that. I didn't make as much as I could have made if I'd been working even at a fast-food restaurant, but I made something. And most importantly to me, no one found out about my pregnancy."

"Did you go to the hospital to have her?" He lifted his shoulder. "I'd always wondered how. I... I hated to think of you alone, scared, and in pain. It's one of my regrets. If I would have known, I'd have been there."

That was sweet of him to say, but she shook her head. "It had nothing to do with you. You didn't need to be there." There was something in his gaze, something in the way he moved his eyes, the way his hand clenched and unclenched, the way he looked away, that made her feel like he didn't agree, but he didn't say anything.

"Mrs. Calvin had a sister who was a midwife. It wasn't ideal, but when I went into labor and refused to go to the hospital, she called her, and she walked us through it. Thankfully, from what I understand, it was an easy birth."

That was not what she wanted to say. She remembered the fear, the pain, the worry that her daughter would die, and the horror that there was a small part of her that hoped she would. Because the problem would be gone. She hated that part of herself. Was embarrassed to even think it, and would never, ever admit that, but maybe that was part of the reason that she had worked so hard trying to become everything she could for the Lord. Not because she felt like she had to earn her salvation. She was clear on that doctrine, but because she felt so terrible for the awful thoughts that she had about the innocent baby in her body.

Garnet sat there, silent, not judging, waiting for her to say more, and the words slipped from her mouth.

"I never considered abortion, but there were times I hoped she died."

She didn't want to say that. Why couldn't she just keep her mouth closed? Maybe it was because she was getting the feeling that Garnet gave her too much credit. She didn't deserve it.

"It would have solved your problems. I think that's a human thing, and it just shows you're human. Wicked and evil and sinful like the rest of us."

With her mouth open, she stared at him. He stared back, totally unperturbed about her deepest, darkest confession.

"I don't think you mean that."

"I know I do. You didn't act on those thoughts. You wouldn't have. But you wouldn't have been human if you hadn't had that thought, that wish that would get you out of the trial you were in, if you hadn't gone through scenarios that would have gotten you out of it. The thing is, you didn't dwell on those thoughts, but took them captive and got rid of them, feeling terrible that they were even there."

He was right. That's what she had done. She knew those thoughts were sin. She knew she had to get them out of her brain, couldn't give them credence in any way, or she would end up being the kind of person she didn't want to be.

"You always looked at me and saw the best. Always," she said softly, the full weight of those memories coming back. He always saw the best in her.

"I just saw what was there," he said simply.

Maybe that was true. It's what he saw, anyway. Because there was only one person she trusted with her baby. Even Mrs. Calvin, who had offered to help her, wasn't her first choice. Not only did she trust Garnet, she knew that Garnet would protect her at all costs. She had been right. He had made the ultimate sacrifice and given his life completely for her baby, making sure that nothing, not a whisper of her origin, had ever been breathed out loud and Mertie had been able to back completely out of the picture. Because Garnet saw the best of her.

Even not knowing where the baby had come from or any details, he looked at her and saw the best.

She moved away, walking toward the water. Studying it, thinking. She'd never actually thought about it, never considered the implications, the idea of what he had done, what he had sacrificed, and what she owed him.

"I can pay," she said suddenly, remembering what he had said about quitting his job and knowing that, while she wasn't a millionaire, she wasn't the penniless, lost girl she'd been. "That would solve your problem!"

Maybe that was the reason God had brought her here! Because the man who had sacrificed his life to raise her daughter needed some of what God had blessed her with.

"I've made enough money that I could live in comfort for the rest of my life. I can keep you in comfort as well. Along with Dabney, of course."

Her name was a little unfamiliar on Mertie's tongue. She tasted it, rolling it around in her head, listening to the sound of it reverberate through her mind, and realizing that that was one more thing Garnet had done. No one knew her middle name. She never used it, she didn't even use the initial. And he had given her daughter her mother's heritage in a way that no one would ever know.

"I owe you more than I ever thought. What can I do to repay you?"

Ten

Garnet stared at Mertie.

She wanted to repay him? How did you repay a person for raising your child for you? For loving her like she was his own, for giving everything he had to make her childhood the best he could. All the while, wishing Mertie was there to give him a hand.

How could she think she could repay him for being a friend?

"No repayment." That was all he could think of to say. There were so many things jumbled around in his head. He didn't want Mertie's gratitude. But he didn't know exactly what he did want. He just... wanted his friend, the friend from childhood, the friend that the years had come between and given them an entirely different perspective on each other and life.

He couldn't have that back. A person couldn't go back and get their childhood back again. It just wasn't done. She had her own life trajectory, and he had his.

"There has to be something. I can pay alimony, only it wouldn't be called that. Something else." Her mind seemed to be whirling.

"I don't want money." He needed to be firm about that, and he emphasized each word. That was not what he wanted.

There was one thing that she could do, not for him though. For the girl he loved more than anything else in the world beyond Jesus.

"Dabney wants a mother." There. He threw it out there, knowing that it was the one thing she wouldn't do. It would destroy everything she had worked for. She wouldn't want the public to know that she had slept with a man she wasn't married to, gotten pregnant, and then given the child up while she ran off, abdicating any responsibility at all.

She had asked him to put the baby up for adoption and entrusted him to do it, and he had. Just hadn't told her that he was the one who adopted her.

"Anything but that," she said, her eyes wide, her stance frozen, her entire being saying she was affronted and offended and shocked that he would even suggest such a thing.

It figured. The one thing Dabney, and he, wanted more than anything was the one thing she couldn't give.

"I'm sorry." Her tone softened, as did the straight line of her body. "It would ruin everything. I mean, not all of my followers would leave. Some people would understand that I made a mistake, years ago, but… I've been offered a position, a position that hundreds, if not thousands of women would love to have, and it was offered exclusively to me. It's huge. Something I absolutely cannot turn down. I would be a fool to do so. It will make my name a household name and elevate my ministry from reaching thousands to reaching millions. Literally. Overnight. The influence that I will have on this country will be almost unheard of. And I can do more for you and Dabney. But I have to be squeaky clean. There can't be a hint of scandal or trouble in my past. Nothing that would disqualify me from giving advice and teaching the Bible to people. I can't have the word hypocrite associated with my name at all."

Garnet watched, meeting her eyes the entire time she spoke. When she finished, he looked down. Those last words, the idea of having "hypocrite" associated with her. Wasn't that what she was doing right now? By not coming forward, admitting that she had made a mistake, admitting that she had a daughter, admitting that she had given that daughter up for adoption…

Wasn't trying to hide that, and trying to pretend that none of that had ever happened, wasn't that the very definition of being a hypocrite?

He pressed his lips closed. Maybe, back when they were teenagers, back when they roamed the beach and the bluffs together, back when he knew her better than he knew himself, he might have pointed that out to her. But now?

"I didn't have any experience with babies at all," he started. Not planning on saying anything, but the words just came to him. "She was so tiny. I was scared I was going to break her."

"I had been shocked at how small she was. I'd never held a newborn before."

"Oh, did you hold her?" he asked as his eyes slipped back to hers.

She nodded. "She was thirty-six hours old when I appeared on your doorstep. I held her and changed her up until that point."

"I'd never fed a baby before in my life. That wasn't too hard. I figured it out. My mom helped me, but there were too many questions here. I had to leave. So I moved out the next day."

"I'm so sorry."

He shook his head. As far as he knew, she had been holed back up in Pastor Calvin's home until the end of the summer. He knew she had a job and she was working out of their home. People just didn't know she was pregnant while she was doing it.

"You left your home," she said, when he didn't speak.

"You made it clear that you needed absolute secrecy. I couldn't stay here. People might put two and two together, although I hadn't realized you were pregnant until you said it was your baby."

"I thought about lying about that. But I just couldn't. I'd like to say that I couldn't lie, but the truth of the matter is, I couldn't lie to you."

That surprised him, but she didn't see the widening of his eyes, because they were still cast down. He nodded his head slowly instead.

"The first time she got sick, I was in my apartment alone. She coughed, and it felt like she couldn't get her breath, and it scared me. I thought she was going to die. I ended up in the ER."

"If I had been with her, it probably would have been just as scary."

"I was afraid I'd lose her. By then, I loved her more than I love myself, and I would have done anything for her. They just laughed at me, told me to give her some Tylenol, told me where to get a vaporizer, and sent us home. I wanted them to admit her."

When he looked up, Mertie was staring at him like she'd never seen that side of him. He hadn't realized he had a side like that or that he could be so scared, so determined to do anything it took in order to save his daughter's life.

"As she grew, she was quiet, sweet, but she has a stubborn streak, and I knew exactly where she got that."

"From me."

He nodded, smiling. Dabney wasn't like her mother at all other than that stubborn streak that wouldn't allow her to stop.

"When I was teaching her to ride her bike, she wouldn't quit. She had fallen, skinning both of her knees. They were bleeding, dripping blood down her leg. But she wouldn't stop. Absolutely refused to stop picking herself up off the ground, and getting back on that bike, and riding it until she had it mastered. Probably that day, for the first time, I truly saw you."

"I suppose there are benefits to being stubborn," she said, sounding subdued.

"Oh, definitely. She doesn't quit things. She learned to read when she was in preschool, because she wouldn't stop asking me to tell her what each letter said and then teach her how to put them together into words. Once she realized there was such a thing, night and day she was after me to help her with words, to sound them out, to figure that reading thing out."

"I guess she gets her intelligence from her father, whoever he is."

"I don't know about that," he said, wondering why Mertie didn't think she was smart. It was true that he had always gotten better grades in school than she had, but she had common sense and people smarts that he lacked. He would have no idea how to climb up the cliffs, maybe that was part of the reason why he quit. He knew he didn't have what it took, but she had the intelligence to figure it out. Had the stubbornness to keep going.

"Do you have more stories?" Her words were soft, but there was a pleading in her eyes that Garnet couldn't resist.

It wasn't exactly his intention to tell her about Dabney and make her want to meet her, long to be a mother to her, but on the other hand, he loved Dabney and wanted the best for her. And he knew that she wanted to know who her mother was, wanted to know why her mother didn't love her enough to keep her. No matter how many times Garnet told her that her mother had reasons and would have kept her if she could, he knew it didn't satisfy her. There was a part of her that felt like there was something wrong with her, or else her mother would have wanted her.

He thought back over the years. He had a million stories. And he loved to talk about his daughter. It was his favorite subject after the Lord. He had a feeling that little snippets of her life would make its way into every sermon he preached. It certainly seemed like it, if this first sermon he was writing was any indication. But what would Mertie like to hear?

"She wants siblings."

That wasn't the top of his list of things Mertie would want to know.

"I bet she does. My sisters were what I clung to when we moved to Chicago and I lost you. I don't know what I would have done without them," she said. "Part of the reason that I came back to help get my parents' house in order was because I wanted to have a better relationship with them."

"She's lonely, I suppose. I have to work. I wish I didn't, but I do, and I can't spend every waking hour with her. She... She'd like to have someone to play with. She'll be fifteen in August, and she's been asking me to get married so I can have children with my new wife, and she'll have babies to watch. She loves kids, loves animals, even reptiles, which... I had to talk her out of the snake that one of her friends wanted to give her."

"A snake? She definitely doesn't get that from me."

"If it breathes, she loves it. Even fish, and in fact, that was one of the earliest things that she ever asked me to do. She wanted to go see the Titanic."

"The Titanic?"

Mertie wrinkled her nose up, and Garnet pointed. "She does that expression all the time."

"What?" Mertie said, wrinkling her nose up again.

"That. That expression right there. You look just like her."

A smile spread across Mertie's face, and she was quiet for a moment before she said, "Why did she want to see the Titanic?"

"She didn't see any fish in the pictures she saw in a magazine. She wanted to go down and see where the fish were. She thought they were shy."

"Really?" Mertie said, looking like she was charmed.

It had been charming. Especially considering that Dabney had only been maybe five years old.

"She was never interested in big crowds and the popular things all the other kids wanted to see. She wanted to go to Alaska so she could see a polar bear."

"Did you explain to her that polar bears are dangerous and that humans aren't supposed to be interacting with them?"

"I gave her an article to read. She figured that out for herself. But she did have a thing for bears for a really long time. Probably from about seven to eleven years old. In fact, her bedroom was decorated with bears. And not cute ones like koala bears or panda bears. She actually found a grizzly bear rug at an old estate auction we went to. Talked me into buying it. It was filthy and sold for a dollar. How could I say no when that was all they wanted for it?"

He laughed. "It cost five hundred bucks to get the rug cleaned. And that wasn't even a professional cleaning, that was just cleaning it up enough to bring into the house. She hung it on her wall."

"On her wall?" Mertie was totally impressed and aghast at the same time. That was the reaction of everyone who heard about that.

Then he realized maybe Mertie didn't know. "I homeschooled her from the beginning."

"Oh." Mertie's mouth closed, and she looked smug. "That explains why she's so odd."

He didn't think that she meant that as an insult, but honestly, one never really knew.

Homeschoolers were odd. In a good way, to his way of thinking, but the rest of the world often thought that they didn't fit in. And it's true, they didn't. But Christians weren't supposed to fit in with the rest of the world, so homeschooling was actually perfect. It produced children that didn't worship at the world's altar. The problem was, homeschooled children were still human, and some rebelled, because they didn't like the feeling of not fitting in. They forgot that this world was not their home, that they were just passing through, that to feel at home in the world, to love it, was to not love God, according to the Bible.

"I'm seeing second-generation homeschoolers in a lot of my meetings. People who were homeschooled and are homeschooling their children. It's...a movement. And while I don't think that you can generalize any group, if there is one group that really understands that the things society loves, the things of the world, the bright and shiny toys that are everywhere around us, are not the things we should be focusing our eyes, attention, or money on, it's that group."

He nodded, knowing that generalizations were dangerous, and he could think of a hundred examples that were not true, but also knowing that if a person wanted to not be in the world and wanted to raise their children to not love the world, homeschooling was probably their best option.

Eleven

"What made you do that?" Mertie asked, and Garnet thought that maybe if she had been a mom, she wouldn't have needed to ask.

"I couldn't stand the idea of sending her to school. Couldn't see doing that, knowing that I was going to have to unteach so many of the things that she was going to learn while she was in the classroom." He hated to admit the next part, because it made him feel like he wasn't a good provider, but it was the truth. "I couldn't afford the Christian school in our town, so that left me one option. Homeschooling. It turned out to be the best option, sometimes God backs us into a corner and we have no choice but to do what He wants. That was one of those times. And I probably needed that, or else I would not have chosen to homeschool. It was the hardest option, requiring the most from me. I love my child, but I wasn't sure I wanted to make the sacrifice, spend the time. Plus, I didn't know if I could."

"Why not? You're so smart. You always got good grades in school. If anyone would be wondering about whether or not they could homeschool, it would be me."

"The grades are just one thing. I wasn't able to teach. I...can never find the right words. You, on the other hand, know almost intrinsically what people need to hear to get them to understand. You know how to...sell things. And I don't mean that in a mean way, I mean that you can break it down, get them interested, bait the hook, so to speak, and break things into small bites that they can understand. I just seem to dump everything in a disorganized way on someone's lap, and they leave shaking their head, frustrated because they're more confused after I talked to them than before."

He laughed, and she laughed along with him, and somehow their shared laughter made the years fall away, and while he didn't feel as close to her as he used to, it didn't feel like there was this huge divide between them that he had felt at the beginning of the conversation. It felt like maybe they could get what they used to have back again.

He caught himself mid-thought. That wasn't the goal. He wasn't trying to get back what they used to have. He wasn't trying to build on that, wasn't trying to have a relationship with Mertie at all. He just... wanted his daughter to know her mother.

And there was a part of him that said that it would be good for Mertie to know her daughter.

She sighed, looking off at the rows of crosses to the right, testament to the son that Vera and Dominic had lost and the other children who were buried in the graveyard by the church.

It was a beautiful graveyard, carefully kept and maintained by Vera and Dominic. They had done an excellent job with it, and in the short time that Garnet had been back in Raspberry Ridge, he had enjoyed the evening walks through the manicured grounds. Someday he would have a headstone somewhere. Unless the people who were left after he was gone decided to cremate him, which he didn't particularly want. It just didn't seem biblical. Although there was no prohibition against it. It just wasn't his preference.

He liked to think of himself in the graveyard, alongside other people who had walked this earth before him or alongside him. Or even after him eventually. All together. Perhaps it would be a little while before he was completely forgotten.

Although, the Bible clearly said this life was like a vapor. Here for a little while and then it vanished away. People weren't supposed to remember him. They were supposed to remember Jesus. That was the point of his life.

How could he do that with Mertie? Help people remember Jesus, especially their daughter.

It made him sad to hear her say that she had a big, important offer that she didn't want to let go of. In his mind, that just screamed something that was not important, one of those red herrings that drew a Christian's attention away from what God actually wanted them to do and onto themselves, their success, their legacy, so to speak.

But who he was he to judge? He didn't know her heart, he only knew his. And it was toward Dabney, wanting the very best for her.

It had always been toward Mertie, wanting the best for her too.

They sat in silence for a while, neither one of them saying anything, and Garnet thought that perhaps their conversation was over.

He didn't mind sitting in silence beside her. They spent plenty of time in their youth studying together, reading together, and even watching TV and movies together. He had been as comfortable with her in silence as he was in conversation.

They definitely didn't have that same level of comfort back, but now that he had spoken with her some, he knew that the same Mertie that he'd known growing up was in there somewhere. This woman, so confident and serene, hadn't seemed like the same girl, but he caught glimpses of her.

"Does she really want a mom?" Eventually Mertie broke the silence with a question that Garnet couldn't have foreseen.

He considered how to answer. He wanted to turn it, to give her an answer that would either make her feel guilty, or pull on a heartstring, or somehow move her to want to be Dabney's mother, but that wasn't the right thing to do. It wasn't right to manipulate people to get them to do what you wanted them to do. Even if what you wanted them to do was a good thing, it still wasn't right.

"Yes. She does."

"Why haven't you ever gotten married?"

He huffed out a breath. "That's a good question."

"I was serious."

"Why haven't you?" He didn't mean to turn the question back on her, but he didn't want to have to answer it. He wasn't sure. He supposed there were a lot of different reasons, and each contributed to the real reason.

"That's easy. Getting married would get in the way of what I wanted. I want to be a Christian speaker and author. I didn't have time to mess around with dating and breaking up and finding someone. And no one looked at me and decided that I was the one and came up and asked me to marry them. Not that I would have said yes, but I would consider that a lot more than I would have considered, 'Hey, you want to go out?'" She looked over his shoulder. "Considering what happened the last time I went out, I wasn't doing that again."

Her voice lost its confidence in volume as she ended, and his heart went out to her. It must be a terrible memory. A terrible experience, something that had marked her, that she would probably take to the grave.

"Have you forgiven him?" He was surprised at the words as they came out of his mouth. But that was the first thing that came to mind when he heard what she said.

"That's a good question," she said, laughing a little but not looking at him. And, he noticed, also not answering him.

"That's a no."

"Are you perfect? Aren't there skeletons in your closet? Are there things that you need to get right with God?"

"Yeah. I need to forgive you."

That made her head jerk around. "You resent me giving you Dabney? But... You said you loved her. I thought you appreciated the fact that you had her. You said that you fell in love with her as soon as you saw her. You could have given her up for adoption."

She talked about Dabney like she was just a thing that he could get rid of if he didn't really want it.

"I could never have done that."

"You should have said something. I could have found someone else. Mrs. Calvin would have been willing. I just didn't know for sure that she would have my back. The way I knew for sure that you would. I never doubted you."

"And you had no reason to. I never said a word." He'd already said that, but it was true. He had never even considered saying a word. He'd done everything he could to protect her. Even though there was a part of him, a part that he didn't want to take out and examine too closely, that had been hurt when she had come to him with someone else's baby. He would never say anything to her about that. After all, it would ruin the friendship that lay between them if there was jealousy there in his heart. Jealousy relating to another man being with Mertie.

"I'm not sure what I did that you need to forgive, but I'm sorry," she said, and he believed she was sincere.

He shook his head. "You didn't do anything wrong. It's just... Sometimes I resented the fact that you took advantage of our friendship, but it only happened because I allowed it, but if I didn't blame you, I had to blame myself, and there were times over the last fifteen years I didn't want to do that."

"No. You're right. I did take advantage of our friendship. I wish I wouldn't have now."

"No!" He wanted to be emphatic about this. "Sometimes, we look at things and we wish that they would have happened differently, and I admit that there were times where I resented the fact that I had a baby to take care of, because it inhibited me from doing exactly what I wanted. But at this point in my life, looking back, I can see that this was the exact best thing for me and God knew it."

"Why do you need to forgive me?" she asked again softly.

He pressed his lips closed. Why indeed? "I suppose there was always a part of me that wanted you and me to raise her together."

Twelve

Mertie stared at Garnet. Was he serious? He had wished that they had been a family together?

That was what he had to forgive her for?

As she considered it, running it over in her mind, she supposed she could see his point of view. He was a single father and could have used a mother's help.

"I know right now you're probably thinking it's through the teenage stage, that change of life where she's asking me about menstruation, and I had to walk in the store and try to figure out what feminine products to buy, and if I wasn't going to talk to her about it, somebody else was going to have to, but I was going to have to talk to them before they could talk to her, and I didn't want to leave it up to just anyone."

"You were homeschooled. You couldn't just let the school do it." That made sense to her.

"No. I couldn't."

If this conversation wasn't so serious, she would be smiling because his cheeks were turning pink underneath his tan. It was cute, except they were talking about her not being there to talk about all the womanly things that her daughter needed to know. They were talking about her leaving him to do it by himself, except she didn't. She had asked him to put her up for adoption.

"Did you ever regret not putting her up for adoption?" she asked, not wanting to rub in the fact that he had brought all of this on himself.

"Lots of times. I wonder what in the world I was thinking. How did I think that a single man could be a mother and father to a young girl, especially one who was growing into womanhood so rapidly. I was so wrong. She would have been better off with a mom and a dad, but every time I thought that, God reminded me that no one would love her the way I did."

And that was the truth. It was obvious that he loved her, loved her with his whole heart, and that was one more thing that Mertie owed the Lord for. He had given her daughter a dad who had loved her more than life. No girl could ask for more. Unless she asked for a mom who loved her the same.

And that's what Garnet wanted. He wanted a mom who loved Dabney more than life. Not just any woman, but one who would love his daughter.

"I dated a little bit. Not much. I couldn't marry someone who was going to treat my daughter like she wasn't their child. I wasn't going to bring anyone home to Dabney that I wasn't completely serious about and intended to make a permanent part of our family. That meant I didn't bring anyone home."

"I'm sorry. You might have had a wife and a whole pile of kids right now, if I hadn't done what I did."

"You pointed out I could have put her up for adoption. But I didn't think it was the right thing to do then, and I'm sure it's not what God wants me to do now."

"I'm not sure of anything." She didn't know whether giving her baby to Garnet had been the right decision or not. Maybe she would never know. "Maybe I should have kept her."

"I would have helped you with her. If you had kept her, I would have raised her with you."

"Two friends don't make a marriage."

"I could have been an uncle. Who said anything about marriage?"

She laughed, embarrassed, and looked away. He was right. He

hadn't asked her to marry him. Not then, not now either. He hadn't even insinuated it. He'd just said he would have raised Dabney with her, helped her. She could have depended on him.

"You didn't love me like that," he said softly as she continued to look toward the water and avoid his gaze.

"And you didn't love me that way."

"I love you."

That made her smile. "I love you too." That was easy to say. It was true. Had she loved him the way a woman loves the man that she wants to spend the rest of her life with? She couldn't remember.

When she had first moved away, they had just been growing into the adults that they would become, and she remembered wondering what it would feel like to kiss him, to stand and lie beside him, but they had never acted on any of those things. When she had given him her baby, she had too many other things on her mind to think about whether or not she had any kind of feelings for Garnet. The idea didn't even cross her mind. At the time, if she remembered correctly, she hated all men.

Stupidly, she figured now, since it was hardly that unnamed boy's fault that she had agreed to have a one-night stand with him. She had known exactly what she was getting herself into, and she hadn't tried to get herself out of it. She had thought that everyone else was doing it and that she might as well too.

The last time she ever thought that.

But all that was water under the bridge.

"Do you think that God brought me here so I can meet you, see Dabney, and... I don't know. Get to know her some?"

"Maybe. Is that what you think?"

"You're the pastor."

"You're the Christian speaker. You write books on these things. What do your books say?"

"My books just point people to the Bible. But that doesn't have an answer to this question."

"Doesn't it? Or maybe we don't want to look for that."

"What do you mean?"

"The Bible has the answer to all of life's questions. We just sometimes don't want to know what the answers are. We don't like them, we dismiss them. They don't suit our narrative or our enlightened views of what society should be, but in reality, man has been doing that since the beginning of time. Rejecting what God says, trying to do things our own way."

"We're like Cain. Giving vegetables as a sacrifice, rather than what God ordained."

"Exactly. Even the first children couldn't just do what God said. They thought they had a better way."

"We think we're different. We think we really do have a better way. We know more now. Science tells us so," she said, sarcasm heavy in her voice.

"Science changes constantly. We make new discoveries, realize things that we thought we knew aren't as right as what we thought they were."

"You found that pattern too?" she asked with a small laugh.

"You'd think it would help me believe the Bible more, but so many times I want to shake my head and say, 'God didn't really mean that. He meant most of the other things in here, but not that.'"

"Or maybe I just skim over it entirely and pretend it's not there. If I pretend I don't see it and pretend I don't know about it, then I don't have to obey."

"Or I remain ignorant of it all and let someone else tell me what they think the Bible says, only they're making up whatever to suit their agenda, and now I'm like one of those sheep who have gone astray, listening to someone other than God and allowing them to tell me what to do."

"It sounds like we both run into this."

"You have more of a ministry than I have though. I just related to it even in our homeschool groups. People scoff when you try to live the way God wants you to."

They were quiet for a moment, and then he said, "It looks like we've taken different paths but arrived at the same place."

She paused a moment to process his words. But then, she thought she understood what he was saying. Their lives had certainly been different, but they agreed on the fundamental principles, the basic principles that govern everyone's lives, and they both agreed that they came from the Bible.

"Interesting how the Lord worked things out that way sometimes," she said softly, wondering what else God had in store for her. He reunited her with her best friend from childhood, showed her her daughter, and gave her the offer of a lifetime, all within the space of a week.

She knew what she needed to say. It had become clear as they spoke. "God's been doing so much in my life lately, I'm a little overwhelmed. I'm also not sure what direction to go, but I do know for sure that I'd like to know Dabney."

"As her mother?"

There was no doubt that there was hope in Garnet's eyes, and she hated to squelch it, but she didn't know about that.

"Once the secret is out, we can't ever put it back."

"Is that how you want to continue to live?" She thought that he might have been pushing her, but then he added, "I'm truly asking. You lived your life that way so far. Surely there must always be a part of you that's afraid that the secret is going to come out and that everything you've built will be destroyed. Especially if it comes out the wrong way. Along with that, I've worried about Dabney finding out. Will she be mad at me? Will she hate me for not telling her? Will she feel betrayed that I knew all along and could have told her any one of the millions of times that she'd asked me, but I chose not to? Will she think that you hated her and didn't want her and that's why you gave her away, and not to push you into anything, but that's how she feels."

She had been listening, but when he said those last words, they ripped her heart right in two.

"I wanted her. I wanted her so bad. But... I hated that boy. I hated him. You're right, I didn't forgive him. Even though he was just doing what he had done with a hundred other girls. He wasn't deliberately singling me out and hurting me on purpose. But it made me mad that he could get away with it, and I was left with the baby to take care of. A body that wasn't mine anymore, and this terrible secret that I've hidden all my life. He hasn't given me another thought. Hasn't given the idea that we might have had a baby together a thought, I'm sure."

"You've allowed him in your life for long enough. I would say kick him out."

"How?" she asked, frustrated.

"Forgive. Let it go."

It sounded so simple. But the whole of her being rebelled against that. Until she remembered that they had just been talking about God's way being best and God's way said forgive. It didn't give parameters on what. Everything should be forgiven.

"So our previous topic of conversation was a really great lead-in to that. Since now I feel convicted. If God's way is right, I need to forgive."

"I wasn't here to beat you up. That wasn't what I wanted," he said, and with those words, he laid a hand on her forearm.

She almost jerked it back. For some reason, some internal part of her knew that it was a bad idea for him to touch her. But he was doing it as a friend. For comfort. To show her that he was sincere.

"I never wanted that," he repeated.

She put her hands up, signaling for him to stop. "I know. I know that. And the same is true of me. I never meant, not in a million years, to put you out, to ruin your life, to—"

He put his hand up and shook his head. "No. I know. And I told you, I wouldn't change a thing."

That wasn't true for her. She would change so many things. Not the least of which would be her stupid, sinful, humanistic desire to be like her friends and think that sleeping around, spending a night with whomever looked good, whoever she had a remote, animal-like attraction for, was okay. Giving her baby away, giving it to her best friend, and infringing on their friendship. It hadn't even occurred to her how much she had asked of him. Even Mrs. Calvin, who had never complained at all, must have done so much to try to keep everything quiet.

All she had been thinking about was herself. From the first moment she set foot out of the door intending on going out with friends, and doing what they did, to the very minute that she walked away from her baby. It had all been about her. Wasn't that what Zebedee Clinger's offer was, too? All about her?

She didn't know where that question came from, but she wanted to deny it categorically. It was about God. Furthering His word. About spreading the gospel to as many people as she could reach.

But wasn't it better for her to take care of her own house first? To take care of the daughter who didn't know whether or not her mother wanted her? And who was hurt because she felt like her mother hated her, that that's why she gave her up. The idea made Mertie's heart hurt.

"Can I meet her?"

"Sure. She isn't the most talkative girl in the world. She enjoys reading and just quietly contemplating things. She also likes to cook."

"Maybe we can have that in common. I've been interested in nutrition and have been trying to make healthier meals for myself, since when I travel, I don't eat very well at all."

"Maybe. She's just trying to find a way around the kitchen. But she is health-conscious."

She couldn't avoid the disappointment on his face, which he tried to hide with an enthusiasm that was obviously fake.

"I really want her to know that I didn't hate her, that I love her and want the best for her, but... Can I just meet her first?" she asked, softly and humbly because if he said no, she would accept it. Although, he hadn't denied her anything. And she had the feeling that he never would. And he wouldn't do it grudgingly or with murmuring or complaining. He truly did want to make whatever sacrifice was necessary in order to do whatever she wanted him to. That was just the kind of man he was.

"Of course. I already told you you could." He paused. "I know you have her best interest at heart. I... I want to avoid hurting her if possible, although I believe, with all my heart, that sometimes we have to go through pain in order to grow, and to learn empathy for others, and to know what other people have to go through in order to forgive us."

"Sometimes we react in anger because someone close to us has gotten hurt, but the best reaction is to teach them how to use that hurt to grow." She had taught that a million times in her seminars and books. It was interesting that Garnet thought the same way. "That doesn't mean I'm going to hurt her on purpose. I promise I'll try as hard as I can not to, but... It's probably going to be a sensitive area for all of us."

"Only if we allow it to be. I think it will be hardest for Dabney because she's a child, but you and I are both adults. We know sometimes life hurts. We also know that we can choose to think the best about people, or we can choose to think the worst. And we know which choice is best."

"Some people don't deserve to have the best thought about them."

"What you deserve has nothing to do with what you get."

He was right about that. So right. If she got what she deserved, she certainly wouldn't have a profitable speaking and writing career, where she got to live for Jesus every single day and point people to Him.

"What do you think would be best?" she asked, wanting to allow him to lead them forward. After all, he was the one who knew Dabney best.

Thirteen

"Can I think about that? Pray about it some?" Garnet took a breath. "I'm not putting you off. I promise. What I really want to do is run to get Dabney right now and introduce the two of you, but I'm pretty sure that that's not the right way."

"I agree," Mertie said easily. Although there was a riot in her chest. She might have just opened up a can of worms that could never be closed. She might have pulled out the nails and started putting them in, the ones that would close her coffin forever, put a lid on the dreams that she had of being an internationally acclaimed speaker and writer.

She had always had big dreams, and she always went for them with all of her heart, but this was one time where she felt like God was leading her in a different direction.

"I'm so glad that you stopped to talk to me. I was sure that God had offered me that position, and I had every intention of taking it, but after talking to you, maybe He was just dangling it out there as something to tempt me away from what I really needed to do."

She gathered herself, pulling up her nerve and realizing she needed to be humble, because she was starting to get the impression that she had made a big mistake.

"I'd like to get to know my daughter. How do you suggest we do it?" Then she added, as an afterthought, "If you think it would be okay."

"I've been telling you I think it's okay. I think it will be wonderful. I know she's going to love you, and I know she wants a mom."

"I'm sorry," she said, feeling like she couldn't apologize for that enough. Even though, she had made the best choice that she possibly could at the time. She had wanted to give her daughter the very best, and the very best was not being raised by a single mom who was probably going to be struggling without money for a long time.

"Again, I just need to think about that for a little bit. I don't want to rush into something and realize that we should have done it a different way. We...might not end up figuring out the best way, but I want it to be perfect, if possible."

She nodded. Appreciating the fact that he wanted to give her the very best shot he could at having a good relationship with her daughter, even though that wasn't what he was saying.

They looked up as footsteps approached.

"That's Homer, recognize him?" Garnet said under his breath as a man pushing a baby stroller walked beside two women, one older and one younger, strolling arm in arm. "And that's his mother and his wife."

"Miss Gertie?" she said, remembering at the last second to keep her voice down.

"The same. Only she's dealing with early-onset Alzheimer's, and she might not recognize you or even remember you."

"That's so sad," she said, remembering she'd heard that at the prayer meeting and feeling a deep sorrow in her chest and an uncanny dizziness in her brain, where the world wasn't quite what she thought it was, and it made her feel off-kilter.

Things changed, people got older, nothing stayed the same, and she knew it, she just didn't always enjoy coming face-to-face with it.

"I'll introduce you if you want me to," Garnet said as he stood.

She moved beside him. "I appreciate that. I recognized him, but he's changed a lot since the last time I saw him."

"I figured." He didn't say anything more as they came up the trail. The older lady pointed out some flowers, and the younger one laughed.

"Hey there, Pastor Garnet."

It was so odd to hear them call Garnet pastor that it took Mertie a moment to realize that they were talking to him. She felt something that was very much like pride go through her. Her best friend, pastor of the church. It was...not totally unexpected. It definitely fit in with his personality, but she wouldn't have guessed. And she wished that they would have spent more time talking about it.

What had made him decide to become a pastor? Why did he move back to Raspberry Ridge? Especially since he mentioned that they weren't going to be able to pay him enough for him to make a living, and he'd have to have another job. So many things that she wished they could have talked about, but instead, he had been typical Garnet, and they had focused on her and her problems. Garnet had always been like that. Putting other people first and giving her a special place. One she really didn't deserve, but he'd always been such a good friend.

"Homer, you probably remember Mertie Jardine, one of the Jardine sisters, who lived up on the hill. She's the oldest, and Amara is the youngest."

Mertie smiled as he introduced her, giving points of reference and mentioning Amara, who Homer was probably familiar with since she'd been back in town for several weeks.

"I remember. It's good to see you," he said, holding his hand out and then indicating the two ladies beside him. "You probably remember my mom. Or at the very least you remember my mom's cookies."

"I sure do. It's good to see you again, Miss Gertie,"

"Who's this?" Miss Gertie said, not in an unkind way, just in a confused, I have no idea who this lady could be kind of way.

"She was a girl who grew up in town here," Homer said easily.

Mertie saw a look pass between Homer and Garnet, and she assumed that Homer was figuring out that Garnet had already told her that Gertie suffered from Alzheimer's and might not recognize her. She supposed that it was probably distressing for Homer since people might be offended that Miss Gertie didn't remember them.

"This is my wife, Skyler, and our daughter, Saylor, who is sleeping and is completely missing the introductions. I'll have to talk to her about greeting strangers."

Homer obviously adored his daughter, something that was easy to see as Mertie watched how he looked at her and heard the humor in his voice. He also adored his wife, as he touched her arm, and a little bit of silent communication went between them as their eyes met, and their lips curved into small smiles.

Mertie always loved watching that kind of by-play between couples who were deeply in love. Not the world's kind of love, lust, but a deep, mutual respect and admiration for each other, that Homer and Skyler obviously had. It was the kind of marriage that Mertie would want for herself if she ever did get married. Not that she had any intention of doing so anytime soon. She was too busy building...

Maybe not. Maybe she had chosen the wrong thing.

The idea didn't sit well with her, and she struggled to make small talk with the group before Homer and Skyler walked away.

"Vera and Dominic designed and built the garden, but Homer supplies electricity for the fountain to run. He also takes care of it as winter comes down and makes sure it's drained before the first freeze of the season."

"So the garden is a community thing?" Mertie said, although she wasn't surprised. It was a small-town thing. Everybody pitched in, because they weren't big enough to have the government to do things for them. And they really didn't need it. When there was an underlying basis of Christianity, people naturally wanted to do the right thing, be neighborly, love each other, and help out.

That was what their country was losing, that underlying biblical basis that prompted people to be moral and to do right.

It was her mission to get it back, and she felt like it was a good one. But maybe she had sacrificed too much in order to do what someone else could do.

She had always thought that she was irreplaceable, but that wasn't true, and she knew it. She just liked to think that, because it made her feel important and needed. But really, the most important place she could be, the place where she was most needed, was in a role that no one else could do. Not as good as she could. Of course, she'd already missed so much of it that maybe it was too late.

"It looks like they thought I might have gotten lost and they needed to come to look for me," Garnet said as they reached the gate of the garden and he held it open so she could walk through.

Lifting up her head, she saw who he was talking about. His parents and Dabney, her daughter. His daughter. Their daughter. Walking down the sidewalk toward them.

The idea was a little odd. Her daughter. Her daughter who Garnet was raising as his.

She wanted to run it over in her head a little bit, get used to the thought, but instead she nodded. "They care about you."

"I moved back into my parents' house so I could help them, and it's almost like my mom thinks I'm a teenager again. I suppose moms never stop being moms—"

He broke off, almost as though realizing what he was saying or who he was talking to. That she hadn't been a mom, and it hurt. She knew he didn't mean her, wasn't insulting her, and in fact had broken off in order to not insult her, but it hurt.

"I'm sorry," he started.

"No. It's okay." She took a breath and put a smile on her face, looking up at him, wanting him to know that whatever she had done, it wasn't his fault. He had done nothing but support her, encourage her, and do whatever he could to take care of someone she loved very much, even if looking back, her actions hadn't shown that.

"Are you going to introduce me?" she asked, unable to stop the wobble in her voice, but she tried to cover it with an even brighter smile. She didn't fool Garnet. His brows drew down, and concern covered his face.

"I wish I could take that back."

"You weren't saying anything that wasn't the truth."

"Sometimes it's better to just keep your mouth shut even if the things you're saying are true."

"You can't walk around on pins and needles scared to death that you're going to upset me. It's my choice as to whether or not I get upset, and I choose not to."

How many times in her ministry had she told people that they could choose what thoughts they were going to think? They could choose what they allow themselves to dwell on, and that would affect their feelings, and feelings were very strong, so a person wanted to be ahead of them. She hadn't quite gotten ahead of those feelings, but she would. She wouldn't allow herself to wallow in self-pity, making the people around her scared to death to say anything that might offend or upset her.

"Are you going to introduce me? I've seen our daughter, but I haven't been introduced." She thought about that short time on the porch when she attempted to go to Bible study but had left, sad. She wished she could take that back too. She had just been overwhelmed and blindsided.

"Of course." He turned, and they walked together until they met up with Dabney and his parents.

"So this is what held you up," his mother said right away, beaming, but also concern on her face. She had her hand hooked in her husband's arm, while Dabney walked on the other side, her arm tucked into his elbow the exact same way.

Mertie remembered that he had suffered a stroke, and perhaps he had trouble walking. There was no walker or cane in sight. Just the ladies helping him. How sweet.

"I suppose I don't usually get distracted by a pretty lady, but it happened to me today." Garnet gave his mom a boyish grin that obviously evaporated any concern or worry she had. "Actually, Mertie is an old friend. You probably remember her. We were practically joined at the hip from the time we were born until the time she moved to Chicago."

"Mertie Jardine?" his mom said, peering at her like her glasses were dirty and needed to be wiped. "Oh my goodness, you've grown into a real beauty. And I've heard that you have quite a ministry."

"Thanks, and thanks again, I guess," Mertie said, wondering where her usual confidence and ability to make anyone feel at ease was. She felt terribly off-kilter and pretty much had all day. "I've really missed Raspberry Ridge. It is good to see it again."

"And this is my dad, Rudy. He probably won't shake, since his stroke has not completely paralyzed his right side, but it's made it difficult for him to move."

"I know Mertie," the man said, his words slightly slurred and a little bit difficult to understand.

"And I remember you, sir," Mertie said gently.

And then her eyes went to Dabney.

"This is my daughter, Dabney. She is the sparkle of the family."

"Dad," Dabney said, rolling her eyes. "I like to read. I never talk. Don't listen to him."

"I think he means it," Mertie said. She could see how he would call Dabney the sparkle of the family, even though she might not talk. She had a way about her that seemed to draw people's eyes. Not in a showy kind of way, just in the kind of way where people enjoyed looking at someone who was soft and sweet and kind.

"But at any rate, it's nice to meet you, Dabney," Mertie said, holding out her hand and waiting for Dabney to pull her arm out from her grandfather's arm and shake.

The girl took her hand with as much confidence as a teen could and gave her hand a perfunctory shake before she pulled it back and took a hold of her grandfather again. Mertie got the feeling that it wasn't because she didn't want to shake her hand, but it was because she didn't want to leave her responsibility of holding onto her grandfather. It made Mertie smile and think that maybe Dabney had gotten a little more than just her stubbornness.

"Launch shoe go home." Garnet's dad's speech was slurred, but Mertie was pretty sure he had just said he wanted to go home.

"All right, Rudy. It's been a pretty long walk, but now that we found Garnet, we can return with a peace of mind," his mother said, carefully nodding at Mertie before she and Dabney moved together to turn on the sidewalk.

"I better go home with them," Garnet said, holding her eyes and seeming like he didn't want to leave. "I'll...be in touch." Not for the first time that afternoon, she had trouble pulling her eyes away. He seemed magnetic to her almost, a pull she wasn't used to, from anyone, much less from the boy who used to be her best friend and who she still kind of thought of as a gangly teen.

But he had grown into a responsible man, a fantastic father, and obviously a dutiful son. As well as a servant of the Lord and pastor of God's word. Shepherd. He would make a good shepherd.

$$Fourteen$$

"Are you busy, Dad?"

Garnet looked up from the porch swing where he had been absentmindedly pushing with one foot while the other leg was stretched out over the swing and his arm hung over the back.

His parents had sat on the porch with him, then he'd helped his mom put his dad to bed. She had gone shortly after, and he had thought that Dabney was reading in her room.

He had a lot of things to think about and had come back downstairs, sitting back down in the dark evening.

"Nope. Come on out and sit with me," he invited, moving his leg down off the swing and shifting in case she wanted to sit beside him. She came out of the door, carefully keeping the screen door from slamming behind her, but chose to sit on the top step, her back against the pole, stretching one long leg out and facing him.

He missed the days when she was young, running out and hopping on his lap, not thinking to assess whether or not he was busy before she did. While he appreciated this older, more considerate daughter, he missed the cuddles and sweet innocence that she was slowly growing out of. But he supposed that was the way life went.

They didn't say anything for a bit, just listening to the chirping crickets and the distant echo of the waves breaking against the bottom of the bluffs. It depended on a lot of different factors whether they could hear the waves, but tonight they were quite clear.

He waited for a while, able to tell from the way she fidgeted that she had something on her mind. Maybe he should have waited for her to figure out how to say it, but he kind of thought that as a dad, it might be his job to ease the way some.

"Did you have something you wanted to talk to me about?" he asked, making his words sound easy and comfortable. Not like he was interrogating her or impatient. She was very sensitive to picking up cues, whether verbal or nonverbal.

"The woman we met today."

It wasn't a question, but she stopped, so he prompted her. "Yeah?"

He couldn't take a deep breath; she would hear him. So he closed his eyes and said a short prayer that God would help him have the right words. He wasn't going to have to think of how he needed to bring Mertie up to her. Dabney was going to ask him something about her and open up a conversation that could potentially be the opening he needed to start a dialogue about her mother.

He wanted so much for his daughter and Mertie to have a great relationship. Just talking to Mertie today, he could see that she wanted to do the right thing, she wanted to make the right choices, and he had never doubted for a second that when she gave Dabney up for adoption, she thought she was doing the right thing. Maybe he had shoved aside the idea that the three of them could be a family. Perhaps there was just a little bit of life left in that idea, and it was a longing in his heart. Distant, and far away, but still with a powerful pull.

"She was the same woman who ran out of Bible study?"

"Yeah."

"Is there something wrong?"

Dabney was very astute, but this was pretty impressive, even for her. Maybe it was the Lord who had put the idea in her head.

"I think she has some choices to make, and while she's here in Raspberry Ridge to help her sisters, she is also here because God has some things He wants to show her."

"Because she wasn't listening where she was?"

"Maybe." He lifted his shoulder, smiling internally. Dabney had listened to him more than what he thought she had.

They were quiet for a bit, and then Garnet couldn't help but ask the question that had been on his mind the entire time.

"What did you think about her?"

It was a little game they played. Dabney had started it. Looking at women and saying why she wouldn't want them as a mother.

It was interesting that most often she picked out the negative qualities, almost as though to make herself feel better. Garnet had noticed that but hadn't known what to do about it.

Dabney tilted her head and put a finger on her chin, as though she were thinking. "She looks so buttoned up. Not like I always pictured my mom. Just... Like someone you would see on TV. A news anchor maybe."

Garnet had to snort, because that was Mertie. Always perfect. Nothing out of place. That was part of the reason why a child wouldn't fit into her life. She didn't have a slot. Not with the direction she was going.

"But there's something else," Dabney began, and Garnet froze. Typically Dabney just said one thing, and they laughed and moved on. "She... She seems like someone who would listen." Dabney took a breath. "And be able to fix things."

Garnet blinked. That was absolutely true of Mertie, and sometimes his daughter's perception floored him.

"Do you have problems that need to be fixed?" he asked, not sure why he said that. Maybe because he just wanted her to talk about it a little bit more. Mertie was one of his favorite subjects, and he didn't often get to discuss her with anyone. Ever.

"I suppose maybe someday I will. But... She would be good for you."

Garnet blinked. He couldn't get his wits about him to say anything more before his daughter stood up.

"I'm gonna run in and see if I can read a couple more chapters before it's time to turn my light out." She didn't wait for him to reply but opened the door, remembering not to allow the screen to slam behind her.

That was the kind of daughter she was. She heard his mother saying not to let the screen door slam, and Dabney always tried to obey the adults around her.

Maybe that's what she was doing now. Maybe Dabney was perceptive enough to know that he was interested in Mertie, and she had something nice to say, some push in that direction. Of course, it didn't negate the fact that she was right that Mertie didn't really seem cut out to be a mom. More like a news anchor or the Christian author and speaker that she was.

Under the cover of darkness, maybe it was easier to allow his thoughts to flow. And even though he knew he should go in and work on his sermon for Sunday, he wondered where Mertie was, what she was doing. Was she looking at the same sky he was, breathing in the lake air, and thinking about him.

He almost snorted again. Mertie didn't waste time on such frivolous activities. And he didn't think that was going to change anytime soon.

Fifteen

"And to sum up, God wants us just the way we are, but He doesn't want us to stay the way we are. If we become Christians, and there's been no change in our life, then there is a problem. And if you are the same person today that you were last year this time, and God hasn't made any changes in your life in the 365 days that have passed, the problem is ours. He is there, He's ready to do the work of sanctification, but we need to allow it, and we need to know what the Bible says in order for us to obey."

Garnet closed his notes as the pianist came to the front.

"I'd like to remind everyone that the altar is open, and if my sermon today did not make sense to you, perhaps it is because you haven't given your life to Jesus." He took a breath. This was not his first altar call, but it was his first altar call in the church where he hoped to spend the rest of his life. As he looked out over the bowed heads, he thought of his own conversion and how he had known that there was sin in his life and that he wasn't a good person. Even though he looked like a good person on the surface.

His eyes almost got caught on Mertie. She was sitting with her sister in the middle of the church, on the aisle.

He didn't allow his gaze to stay but tried to focus on mankind's need for salvation and his responsibility in this small corner of the world.

"Christ came to the world to save sinners, of which I am chief," he said, paraphrasing Paul's words. "If you'd like to follow Jesus, but you've never accepted His free gift of salvation, never had your sins forgiven, cleansed by the blood that He shed on the cross, never repented of your sins and come to a saving knowledge of Christ, and don't know for sure that you will spend eternity with God, you can certainly come to the front and I would love to talk to you about it."

The pianist began to play softly, and he added, "If you are convicted by the sermon today and you'd like to come forward and talk to the Lord about that, the altar is open, and you're welcome."

As he spoke, he straightened his notes on the pulpit and then made his own way to the altar. God resisted the proud but gave grace to the humble. He always felt like kneeling at the altar, bowing his head and heart before God and in a show of humility, was good for him. Not to mention, there weren't too many times in his adult life where he hadn't had at least something that he needed to talk to the Lord about.

He knelt at the altar, alone, as the pianist continued to play. He assumed she would play until he told her to stop or until someone else did. But in the meantime, even if no one joined him, he would spend a few minutes talking to God. Thanking Him for this opportunity and asking that His will be done in the hearts and minds of the people who needed to vote next week after his second sermon.

He was in the middle of telling God that he wanted his own life to change. That he didn't want to be the same today as he was last week, that he wanted to be even closer to the Lord next week, when he felt movement at his side.

The light blue skirt and white blouse that Mertie had been wearing came into his peripheral vision.

She didn't touch him, but she knelt down beside him, her face bowed low, her hands on the small rail in front of her as her forehead bent, touching them.

She didn't pray aloud, and she didn't acknowledge his existence, but her presence beside him bolstered his spirit. Whether she had been touched by the sermon, or whether she had just felt bad for him kneeling here alone, he wasn't sure. But her movement must have sparked others, because air swished behind him as someone moved, and he could see from the other side to other forms kneeling at the altar.

He didn't have grand dreams of bringing the United States to revival, but he did hope and pray that even if he wasn't sworn in as a pastor here, that his messages would stir the hearts of Christians, causing them to reevaluate their lives, look at places that they could improve, and cause them to desire to be closer to the Lord. Even in this small church, with this small congregation, revival could change things.

G arnet was good.

Not just good, he was an amazing pastor. An amazing preacher. Outstanding at opening up the word of God and applying it, speaking in such a way that she could apply it to her life easily.

Mertie wasn't sure she had ever heard anyone better.

In fact, she knew she hadn't. The wisdom and depth to Garnet's sermon, while still being simple enough to be easily understood and interesting enough to keep her attention for the entire forty minutes that he spoke, amazed her, astounded her, and stirred something in her that made her want to be closer to him.

When he had gone up to the altar by himself, it had taken her all of half a second to know that she wanted to join him there. Whether it was because the sermon had stirred her soul so much, or whether she just wanted to somehow show him by her presence that he changed her life in the last forty minutes, she wasn't sure.

He hadn't preached anything profound, just that as Christians they should continue to grow.

As she stood from the altar and moved back toward her seat, carefully avoiding looking at Garnet, because it wasn't an appropriate time for her to speak to him, her eyes met the eyes of someone in the back. Someone she hadn't seen around town, and someone who...just seemed to be searching.

So, after the congregation was dismissed, and Garnet moved to the back to greet people, Mertie hurried from her seat and walked around to the back corner, where she had seen the girl, young lady, looking at her.

She caught her just as she was getting out of her pew and stuck her hand out.

"I'm Mertie Jardine." That's all she said, hoping that the girl wouldn't walk away from her.

She was older than Mertie had first thought. Maybe mid twenties. She looked at Mertie's hand for a full three seconds before her own came out.

"I'm Becky," she said softly.

Her hand was callused and rough, the hand of someone who worked manual labor for a living, but her grip was strong and her eyes met Mertie's as they shook. She didn't give a last name.

"I'm new here in town, so I don't know everyone, but I haven't seen you before," Mertie said, not bothering to explain that she had grown up in town, left, and was now back hoping to clean out her parents' house and sell it.

"I grew up...in Strawberry Sands," Becky said with an odd pause, like she, too, was leaving out a lot of her life story.

"That's not far from here. Did you just move up the beach a little?" Mertie said, wondering how she could bring the conversation around to anything that might be helpful to Becky. She seemed like a lost soul.

"No. I...moved away for a while."

"Found a better job somewhere else?" Mertie prompted, knowing that one of her strengths was typically having the right words, being able to put people at ease and talk to them in a way that related to them.

"No. I needed to get away for a while."

"Broken heart?" Mertie said gently, instinctively feeling like this was the problem.

"I suppose you could say that."

"But you just can't stay away from Lake Michigan?"

Mertie almost said that as a statement. She could feel the call of the lake too. There was just something about it that drew her. Maybe it was the way she felt every time she looked at it, like God was so big, so amazing, it just reminded her of the power and glory and might of the Lord. She never felt like she worshiped God like she did when she was beside the lake.

"I suppose." Becky didn't say anything more, and Mertie didn't push her.

"Are you settling down here?" she asked easily.

"I think so. There's a small property for sale just up the beach, and it has a horse stable and some pasture."

"Oh. You're a horse lover," Mertie said, seeing the spark in Becky's eyes when she talked about horses.

"I am. I didn't realize it until I was almost a teenager, but yeah. Horses speak to my soul, they point me to God. They remind me of how much our Creator loves us, that He would make something so beautiful and then allow us to take care of it." She looked down and shuffled her feet a bit. "I suppose I'd forgotten that."

"We humans have a tendency to forget. Even things that are right in front of us, things that we think we'll never forget, we're just...prone to wander."

She could say that in her own life. That she forgot that people were the most important thing, and not her career, people like...Dabney. And like Garnet. And even Becky. Mertie couldn't deny that she felt a strong pull toward the girl, all the while there was a voice in the back of her mind saying that it didn't matter how many millions of people she reached, if she neglected the people she loved.

She heard some whispers about the new preacher and the fact that he had a daughter and no wife. Apparently Garnet had not told them she was adopted, and people were whispering, wondering what his marital status was and where Dabney had come from.

Or maybe Garnet had told people, but the gossip hadn't made its way around. She wasn't sure.

"I'd love to see you again. I'll be here for a while. In fact, I'm thinking about staying," she said, surprised as the words came out of her mouth. The idea of staying was...new.

"If the sale goes through, I'll be here. And...it's been a while since

I've been to church. I need to come back. It will make my...parents happy."

She stumbled over the word "parents," like again, there was more to what she was saying than the words she put out in the air.

So true for a lot of things. People often didn't say everything they thought. Usually there was more. Mertie had figured that out, and she had become somewhat good at drawing the information out of people. But she didn't want to do that today with Becky. Part of drawing information out of people was knowing when to quit so that there was still an opening for the next time.

"I'll see you around, Becky," she said, thinking about putting her hand up for another handshake, but instead she put her arms out as though she was going to hug her, and Becky's eyes widened before she submitted to Mertie's embrace, even returning it.

Becky walked away, and Mertie followed her with her eyes, feeling her heart tugged toward the girl who just seemed to have a tragic air about her. She said a quick prayer, that God would draw her to Him, and He would heal her broken heart.

"Hey, I just want to make sure that you remembered that I'm going to Hobert's to eat today. You're welcome to come if you want to."

Her sister, Amara, appeared at her side.

"Oh. Yes. Go right ahead. Have a great time. I'm going to stay home," she said, not that she had any great plans, but she knew Hobert had a couple of late nights fishing this week, and Amara hadn't seen him much. She didn't want to be the third wheel, although Amara and Hobert had never made her feel that way.

"Are you sure?" Amara asked, looking deep into her eyes.

Hobert appeared at Amara's elbow, slipping an arm around her and saying, "You're welcome. Please don't feel like you're not."

"I know I am," Mertie said. But she also knew that they needed some time together. "Maybe we'll have supper together sometime this week."

"If I can get you to stop working long enough to eat," Amara said, giving her another long look before she squeezed her arm, and the two of them walked off.

Mertie knew that she had a tendency to throw herself into things, giving her entire being to the work that was in front of her.

She thought that it was mostly a good thing, but sometimes she could get a little dogmatic about stuff. Like building her career. She had built it at the expense of everything else, even checking in with Garnet to see whether her daughter had been adopted or not. It hadn't even occurred to her that he might adopt her himself. But now that she knew it, she just couldn't go back to living the way she had. She wanted to be a part of her daughter's life, and she knew that Garnet wanted that.

The problem was, the more she thought about it, the more she wanted to be a part of Garnet's life too, and their relationship had never been that way. They had just been friends.

Still, she lingered in the church, straightening some hymn books and talking to a few folks while the sanctuary cleared out.

With the small congregation, it didn't take terribly long, and soon Mertie found herself alone, standing in front of Garnet. She had paid attention to Dabney and knew that she had walked home with Garnet's parents.

"That was an amazing sermon. Possibly the best sermon I've ever heard, and I've listened to more sermons than the average American," she said, unable to not give him the compliment she felt he deserved.

His eyes opened, and so did his mouth, surprised at the words she spoke.

He had always been modest and humble, but he truly didn't seem to know that his sermon was extraordinary, his wisdom unusual, and his ability to simplify things uncanny. Not to mention the fact that the entire thing had been interesting.

"Thanks."

"It's not easy to get people to sit for forty minutes and listen to something anymore. Especially to just one person, but you did it easily, at least it appeared to be with no effort. I was impressed," she said, sincere.

"Thanks for coming today. And I know you didn't come to the altar for me, but it definitely was encouragement to me, and I think that other people just needed to see someone go first."

"You're right, it really wasn't for you, but it was because of you. I'm not kidding about how I felt about your sermon."

He smiled, and she realized that they had shaken hands, and their joined hands were still between them.

She looked down, her first instinct to yank her hand back but then wondering why he hadn't let go.

"Would you like to eat lunch with us? My parents are going to take a nap, but I promised Dabney we'd eat on the beach."

"I don't want to interfere with daddy-daughter time."

"You're the mom," he said, softly. But the words pierced her conscience, and even though she'd been thinking about being a mom for a few days, they seemed to awaken something else in her.

The words seemed to settle between them, and she wasn't sure whose turn it was to talk.

"I don't want to force you, but you're welcome to come." He hesitated, then he looked over at the disappearing form of his daughter and parents. His mom on one side of his dad, his daughter on the other. Maybe there was a bit of pride in his gaze when he looked back at her.

"Dabney said that you would be good for me."

Her brows went up. She couldn't help it. "She did?" Astonishment clear in her words.

"She did. I was kind of surprised myself, but she said she thought you seem like the kind of person who could fix things, the kind of person I could talk to."

"We always talked. Although, I think I did more talking than you did."

"I didn't tell her we used to be friends. Maybe that was why. We were compatible, even though most people wouldn't look at us and think so."

"I don't know. Being that I'm a Christian writer and speaker and you're a pastor, we probably have more in common than what we think. Our personalities are just a lot different."

She never thought about their differences, never thought about why they might be friends, but he was right. Their similarities bound them together, while their differences enabled them to bolster each other's weaknesses. The idea floated through her brain that they were absolutely perfect for each other.

"You can say no. It's okay."

It took her a moment to bring her mind back to what they were talking about.

"Lunch? I want to, I just don't want you, or more especially Dabney, to resent me. I don't want to interfere if this is something special for the two of you."

"I wouldn't ask you if I thought it was going to be a problem. Dabney likes you. She never said anything like that about any of the other women we talked about before."

"You talked about women before?"

"She wants a mom. We talked about what kind of woman would make a good mom. You've garnered more compliments than any other woman we talked about. In fact, you're the only one who garnered compliments. Usually she goes out of her way to make sure that I know that she's happy with just a dad. But I know she's not."

His words were not intended to make Mertie feel bad, but they did. The reason she didn't have a mom was because of Mertie. But if Mertie had kept her, she wouldn't have had a dad.

"I'll go. I don't have a chair or anything like that."

"We have a blanket that we usually use. It's...casual." His eyes seemed to hold more information than what he was saying.

She looked at his gaze, wondering what he was hinting at, if anything. Maybe he was just thinking about something else.

Finally, she said, "Is there something you're not telling me?" She tilted her head, narrowing her eyes a bit as she tried to figure out what in the world he could be saying.

Then she realized his hand was still holding hers, and his thumb ran over the side of her hand.

She looked back down at their joined hands. They had definitely been joined way too long to be excused as anything other than...what? What could be the reason?

Why hadn't she pulled her hand away? She wasn't sure she could give a cognitive answer. Because she liked him holding it? Because it felt good and right for her hand to be in his? Because she was seeing him as something other than her childhood best friend?

"It's okay to loosen up sometimes." He grinned. "Part of what I love about you is how you're always on top of things. You always seem to have everything under control, and you're not afraid to dig in and fix what isn't. But... When you let your hair down, that side of you that no one gets to see, I love that side too."

His words sent a shiver down her torso and made her neck hairs prick.

There was a side of her that he loved? No, by his words, there were two sides that he loved.

"I've only been back in town for a few days, beyond that, it's been more than a decade since we saw each other. You can't possibly know what you love about me." It was her best scholarly voice.

"Really?" he said simply. He didn't argue with her, didn't try to prove that he was right, just questioned her assertion, which of course made her question it too, because how could she tell him what he did or didn't love? Obviously that was what he was saying, and he was correct.

She didn't know. She did know she wasn't the same person she was as a teenager, but she was very similar. All the tendencies that had been there when she was young, all the things she had wanted to do, were still right there, she was just a more mature version of herself, a few mistakes under her belt, but more successes as well. If she looked at success the way the world defined success. She found her definition seemed to be evolving.

"You want me to meet you on the beach?"

"You can come with me. We can walk there together. That would be more time together."

It was like he wanted to spend time with her. Her heart did two extra hard thumps before it settled back down in her chest. Her fingers still buzzed. He wanted to spend time with her? That's what it sounded like.

She tried to calm her racing thoughts and give a dignified nod.

She knew he had to be careful because he wasn't going to be with anyone Dabney didn't accept. He didn't need to tell her that, she just knew it.

"I need to close the church up. They've given me the key for now." He gave that grin that was boyish and self-deprecating and that made her heart do a slow flip.

"Small towns."

Her smile matched his. She forgot about the charm of small towns. There was so much love and so much that made her wish that this was where her home was, rather than the big city, where she was never going to walk into a church one day and have them give her the key to the place, trusting her implicitly.

Raspberry Ridge was absolutely perfect.

Seventeen

S he hadn't pulled her hand away, so after Garnet had locked up the church, he walked down the steps where Mertie stood, looking out over the graveyard and the view of the lake beyond, and slipped his hand back into hers.

She startled a little but didn't pull away. He smiled to himself. He didn't know what that meant, maybe that she was a little bit at loose ends and just wanted his support, but where he came from, friends didn't hold hands.

That's where she had always placed him and where he had been content to stay for a while, but now that she was back in his life, he didn't think that God had done that just for them to renew their friendship.

Maybe.

But that wasn't what he wanted, and while he thought it was dangerous to hope that God wanted the same thing he wanted, he had been praying hard for that very thing.

Whether he became the pastor here in Raspberry Ridge or not, he definitely wanted to pursue whatever this was with Mertie and not let this second chance slip away.

He shouldn't have allowed her to walk out when she gave him

Dabney. He should have at least stayed in touch, but he couldn't change the past. All he could do was seize the future with both hands and not allow himself to squander another opportunity.

"I've forgotten how beautiful summers are here beside the lake," she said as they walked along the sidewalk.

"Same. Summer has always been my favorite, but there's just something about that lake breeze and maybe the reflection of the sunshine on the water."

"Watching thunderstorms roll across the lake. That's pretty awesome," she said softly. "It just shows you how majestic and powerful God is."

"I have to agree. There's something about the lake that reminds you of God's glory and majesty." He felt it so much more when he was in Raspberry Ridge than anywhere else in the world. He couldn't be here without being reminded of it every single day. "I hope I don't ever take that for granted."

"It's true, sometimes we do have a tendency to take things that we get every day for granted. My friends."

He kept his mouth closed. He wasn't sure what she was saying. They were friends. Did she have someone in particular in mind? Or was she just giving an example, because she was correct. People often took their friends for granted.

"Our spouses." He'd seen that a lot in his ministry as well. People taking their spouses for granted, just expecting them to do things because they were married and not giving them the gratitude that they deserved.

"Parents, family, small towns. I definitely took my small town for granted and left without a backward glance. Being back here has definitely opened my eyes to things that the big city doesn't offer."

"A globe-trotting lifestyle doesn't offer either," he said softly.

"Is that why you've chosen to candidate for pastor of a small town?" she asked, refusing to allow his words to apply to her.

"I suppose. I didn't exactly have a globe-trotting job before this, but yeah. Small towns need pastors just as much as big towns, and while I suppose the lure of having a big church and making a big name for myself is there, I know that's vanity."

"Really? You don't think reaching lots of people with a big ministry isn't a worthwhile pursuit?"

He chose his words carefully, because he didn't want to insult her, and he also didn't want to sound like he was trying to influence her to do what he did or to sound like he was saying that what he had done was better.

"I definitely think big ministries are worthwhile pursuits. Reaching as many people as you can for Christ. If that's what God has for you. But sometimes, God just wants us to brighten our little corner of the world."

He hummed a bar, then he started singing and she joined him in harmony.

Do not wait until some deed of greatness you may do,
Do not wait to shed your light afar;
To the many duties ever near you now be true,
Brighten the corner where you are.
Brighten the corner where you are!
Brighten the corner where you are!
Someone far from harbor you may guide across the bar;
Brighten the corner where you are!
Just above are clouded skies that you may help to clear,
Let not narrow self your way debar;
Though into one heart alone may fall your song of cheer,
Brighten the corner where you are.
Here for all your talent you may surely find a need,
Here reflect the bright and Morning Star;
Even from your humble hand the Bread of Life may feed,
Brighten the corner where you are.
Brighten the corner where you are!
Brighten the corner where you are!
Someone far from harbor you may guide across the bar;
Brighten the corner where you are!

They had made it to his parents' porch, and he kept a hold of her hand as they stepped up. There was a part of him that was a little embarrassed that he was living with his parents. Shouldn't a man be more successful in his life? Shouldn't he have his own home and a thriving career where he made a lot of money, rather than bringing the girl he was interested in to his parents' house and knowing he didn't even have a job with which he could support her.

Even while he was bothered by that, he knew that he was exactly where God wanted him. He was doing what the Lord willed, and while it didn't really look successful in the world's eyes, his definition of success wasn't supposed to be the same as the rest of the world's.

He opened the door, allowing Mertie to walk in first. She was not unsure and carried herself with her usual confidence, every hair in place, despite the stiff breeze that had been blowing, her blue pencil skirt pristine and perfectly pressed. Her white blouse with not a smudge on it.

She wasn't exactly dressed to go to the beach. He felt a little bad bringing her along, especially considering how nice her clothes were. He should have suggested she go home and change.

"Rudy decided he wanted to go take a nap on the couch, and he barely lay down before he was snoring," his mom said as she met them by the opening to the living room, where his dad snored on the couch.

"Nice that getting him to bed was so easy," Garnet said, feeling bad that his mom had such a difficult job, caretaking for his dad. He helped where he could, but... Maybe she would want to go to the beach today.

"Dabney is upstairs changing. She's so excited. You guys are going to have a picnic on the beach like we used to."

"Good times," Garnet said. Then he indicated Mertie. "We asked Mertie if she'd go with us, and I figure there's probably more than enough food for an extra person."

"You know I always pack a lot. We had such good times," his mom said. He wasn't always a great judge of what people were thinking or feeling, but it seemed pretty obvious to him that his mom was a little sad that she would be staying home to care for his dad.

"I hope you all have a great time. I'm so glad you were able to go. When Garnet came back, it just wasn't the same when you weren't around, since you guys were inseparable when you lived here."

She held her arms out, and Mertie stepped in for a hug. Then she pulled back.

"What if you go for a picnic with them? I can stay here and keep an eye on Mr. Rudy. I don't know how many times I've crashed your kitchen and you guys fed me or packed a picnic and sent us off to explore the beach. I certainly owe you."

"Aww, I wouldn't dream of it. I'd love to go, but—"

"Then go. I'm kind of overdressed for a picnic on the beach anyway," Mertie said, indicating her nice outfit.

Garnet wanted to step in. He wanted Mertie to go, but the way his mother's eyes had lit up, the way the tiredness had seemed to lift off her face, the way she smiled, thinking about all the good times they'd had on the beach, he couldn't indicate by word or deed that he would rather go with someone else.

"Are you sure?" she said, looking at Mertie's outfit. "Although that is kind of nice to be sitting on a blanket in the dirt and pebbles."

"I know. If I would have realized I was going for a picnic, I would have dressed a little differently."

Garnet doubted that she owned a single thing that would be appropriate for a picnic on the beach. Although she'd been working on the house, painting and such, and he supposed the outfit she'd worn to Bible study was the closest to old clothes she had, and she still looked amazing in his opinion. It was a little hard for him to imagine her as looking anything but perfect. As much as he knew that was wrong.

"Is there anything I need to know?" Mertie said as she peeked into the living room again. "Medicines that he needs to take or anything I should make sure happens when he wakes up?"

His mother rambled off the times for his meds and led Mertie to the kitchen to show her a list taped to the refrigerator door.

Garnet followed, coming face-to-face yet again with the fact that his father was growing old. Of course his mother was too, and he should thank Mertie for stepping back and allowing her to be able to get out. It had been a long time since he and Dabney had gone anywhere with his mother, and the conversation that he had with Mertie on the way home from church, about them taking advantage of the people closest to them, rang in his head. Soon, he wouldn't have his mother to do things with, and he knew he should be cherishing every moment he had with her.

His sermon seemed apt at that moment as well, since he had extorted his congregation to be better than they had been even a week or a month or a year ago. This was one of the areas where he could improve.

Of course, that didn't negate the fact that he wanted to spend as much time as he could with Mertie.

Maybe once they came back, she would have time for him.

He got the cold drinks and a pack of ice out of the refrigerator and finished packing the basket that his mom had sitting on the table while Mertie and she had a conversation in the corner.

He heard Mertie saying that she would help wherever she could and that perhaps they could even have their own morning prayer meeting at her house, so she wouldn't have to worry about leaving her husband.

Garnet didn't know why he hadn't thought to ask if they could move the prayer meeting to his home, other than Homer had been the one to start it, and his mother was in failing health as well, dealing with Alzheimer's.

There she was, stepping in and fixing things, the way Dabney had noticed right off.

"Are we ready to go?" Dabney came into the kitchen, her eyes shining, her clothes changed, carrying a beach towel.

"I am, if your dad's ready," his mother said immediately.

He nodded, and Helen came over, linking her arm with Dabney as they walked down the hall.

"I kinda wanted to spend some time with you," he said as Mertie leaned against the counter, smiling at him.

"I think this'll make your mom happy. She looked tired and a little sad."

"You're right." Thinking again about how she had seen that, when he hadn't. "I guess I was being selfish, wanting you."

"There will be other times for us," she said with confidence.

"Will there?" he asked, knowing that she wasn't staying forever. If he was going to get to spend time with her before she left to go back to her big-city position, he couldn't mess around.

"Yes. I'm sure of it. Go on, enjoy some time with your mom and your daughter."

"I kind of wanted you to be able to spend some time with her too."

For some reason, his feet didn't want to take him out of the house. They wanted to stay right where Mertie was.

"I want to too. But I know I did the right thing."

He couldn't argue with that. He just nodded, grabbed the basket which was heavier than he expected, and turned toward the door.

"Can I leave my number, just in case?"

"Sure. Tell me what it is, and I'll program it in."

He rattled it off, watching as she typed it in, and then his own phone dinged.

"I just sent you a text, so you have my number too. I'll be sure to let you know if I have any trouble."

"All right. That makes me feel a little better."

"Go on. Get out of here. Have a fun afternoon."

She made shooing motions with her hands, and while he thought that maybe she looked a little bit sad that she wasn't going, she had the smile of someone who knew that they were doing something nice for someone else, and they were enjoying that feeling. He didn't want to take that away from her. So, with a nod of his head, he hefted the basket and walked out of the house.

Eighteen

Mertie was right, Garnet did have a good time, and he was sure that his mom did too. Thankfully she wore a hat, because she had barely been outside at all, since she'd spent so much time caring for his dad. It made his soul smile and warmed his heart to see his daughter and his mom having such a good time together. His daughter even convinced his mom to wade in the lake, although she didn't actually go swimming. He and Dabney spent some time in the water, and they even got a kite in the air that his mom had stuck in the picnic basket.

In all, it was three hours until they stepped back up on the porch, but Mertie had used the three hours constructively, if the scent of chocolate chip cookies wafting out the front door as he opened it was any indication.

"I smell cookies!" Dabney said, looking first at him and then at her grandmother.

"I do too!" his mom said, and he wasn't sure who sounded more excited. "I can't remember the last time I had homemade chocolate chip cookies that I didn't have to make myself."

"You guys better get going in the house, or I might run you down in order to get myself in there, because if there are cookies in there, I think I ought to be testing them, just to make sure they're safe."

It was a common line, maybe a dad line, but the ladies in his life laughed as he held the door open and they walked in.

Both of them knew he wouldn't run them over to get anywhere, even out of a burning building, but they laughed along at his joke anyway.

As they walked into the kitchen, Mertie stood up from where she was bending over the stove, a tray of cookies in her hand.

"I'm not sure whose apron this is, but I hope it's okay that I borrowed it."

It was a pink frilly one and looked like one that his mom had had for Dabney years ago when she was still small. It barely covered much of anything, but Mertie somehow made it look cute and stylish at the same time. Maybe that was just what happened to clothes when Mertie put them on. The way she carried herself, the confidence that exuded from her, the caring and compassion that underlined everything she did, couldn't help but make her attire look professional and casual at the same time. Or maybe he was just biased, and everything she did was perfect to him.

He had a feeling that the latter was true.

"Can I have a cookie?" Dabney asked, and Garnet looked down at her. She seemed eager, almost childlike, when normally she seemed reserved and mature. She was acting her age, and he wondered what it was about Mertie that drew that out in her.

"Of course. I was hoping you guys would eat them. I certainly can't eat all of these myself. I'll be sick as a dog if I try to do that."

She waved a spatula over the counter at the far end.

"Those are the first ones I took out, so they should be the coolest. But if you want one that's still warm, you might want to choose one from here." She waved her spatula over the middle cookies, and that's where Dabney chose. His mother had gotten plates and handed one to Dabney and then one to him.

"I think I'm going to take two," she said as she did just that. "I take it Rudy didn't wake up?"

"He did for a little bit. He seemed confused, but when I told him you guys were at the lake, that seemed to calm him down and he closed his eyes. I kind of wonder if he'll even remember waking up when he actually does get up from his nap."

"He probably won't. He's used to me being there all the time, and it probably was concerning that I wasn't sitting beside him."

"He did seem a little scared at first, but he settled right down once he heard me talk about the lake. I guess you guys have been living beside it long enough that those words penetrated."

"That makes sense," Helen said as she nodded at the door. "Dabney and I are going to go sit on the front porch for a little bit."

She smiled at him as she went out, and Garnet wondered if maybe she had an idea which way the wind was blowing.

She hadn't said anything at all while they were sitting at the beach, but Dabney had been with them almost the entire time, or maybe she just hadn't wanted to interrupt their interlude and her very rare bit of time away.

"If I didn't know better, I think I just got permission from my mom to stay in here and talk to you."

She laughed. "I don't think you need permission. She knows that you and I were pretty much joined at the hip since we've been born."

"There were a few years where I didn't know where you were, and I assume you had no idea what I was doing."

"Right," she said, her voice totally devoid of the humor that it had held just seconds ago.

He hadn't meant to make her sad or even to push the conversation in a serious direction. He wanted to laugh with her. But he also wanted her to know that friendship wasn't all he wanted.

He wanted to think they had plenty of time, except... They didn't. She would be leaving.

"How long do you think you're going to be here getting your parents' house ready to sell?"

"I'm not sure. My middle sister, Olive, hasn't even made it here yet. Amara is pretty wrapped up with Hobert, but she also doesn't want to do too much without Olive approving it, even though Olive said she didn't really care. You know how that goes, you throw out the one thing that they wanted to keep. And then you hear about it for the rest of your life."

"Yeah." Maybe he was a little distracted, because he was busy saying a prayer that Olive wouldn't come for a very long time, since it sounded like that was the only thing that was going to keep Mertie around.

She seemed to hesitate. "If I'm going to accept the offer I have, I'll have to leave soon. And they'll just have to deal with things without me."

He swallowed. That could mean she'd leave this week.

"Have you talked to Doyle since you've been back?" Mertie asked, filling out the next tray with cookie dough as she spoke and not seeming to realize she'd shifted his world.

"Doyle McKenny?" he asked, surprised that she would mention him, and to his chagrin, a little bit of jealousy squeezed at his heart until he remembered that Doyle and Olive had been like Mertie and him. Best friends, constantly together.

"Yeah. I thought Olive would be excited to come back and see him. Surely he's grown up by now."

"I actually heard that he made some great moves in the Chicago real estate market, and I believe I heard he's a billionaire now. I don't think he's going to show up in Raspberry Ridge anytime soon."

Mertie looked disappointed but not crushed, and he was pretty sure that her interest was purely for her sister's sake.

"I always thought that Olive held the torch for him. When we moved, I lost you, and she lost Doyle. I seemed to handle that kind of thing better than she did, and I felt like she always wished that we could go back. Then when we finally did, Doyle was gone. I think she wouldn't mind seeing him again."

"I know seeing you again has been really nice for me." That really wasn't on the subject, but he wanted to spend the time they had talking about them, or their relationship, or at least their daughter. Even though he wasn't the father, biologically, he was still her father, and Mertie was her mom. She was their daughter.

Mertie put the tray in the oven, closed the oven door, and stood with her back to him for a moment. He hadn't moved from where he stood at the table after setting the picnic basket down by the floor.

Slowly she turned around to face him.

"Seeing you has been really nice for me too. In fact, seeing you and talking to you has made me reevaluate exactly where I was in my life."

She paused for a moment and then slowly walked across the kitchen floor, putting a hand on the chair beside him, leaving a distance between them, which he longed to close, to touch her, to have some kind of physical connection.

"I think I mentioned to you that I had just been offered... The biggest opportunity in my career landed in my lap, and I thought only a fool would say no. But... I've been struggling really hard with what to do."

He couldn't stop the thrill that leapt inside of him, that she was even considering something other than seizing the biggest opportunity of her career with both hands.

"What do you think the Lord wants you to do?" He knew that was what he needed to say. It wasn't what he wanted to say, but it was the right thing.

"I'm not sure. I just think He brought me here to Raspberry Ridge, brought me back to you, knowing that...you have wisdom, discernment, and an ability to see things that I don't. That was brought home to me during your sermon today."

He didn't feel wise. He didn't feel exceptionally discerning either. She had complimented his sermon, which he appreciated, but he wasn't sure if she had meant it. What she was saying now said to him that she truly had.

"I don't think, if I were you, I don't think I would trust anything I say in regards to what you should do with your future." There, that was the honest-to-goodness truth and maybe a warning too.

"Why?" she said, tilting her head, her fingers playing with the back of the chair. "I trust you. I know you're not going to tell me to do something that you don't think I should or that you think would hurt me."

"No. But I might be selfish. I might have an ulterior motive. Might want you to do something that is not what God wants you to do. He is definitely not selfish, and He doesn't have any ulterior motives, other than your good and His glory."

"You mean you have another motive other than God's glory?"

"Sometimes I want things. As a man. A human."

"I didn't know pastors had feelings."

He knew she was joking, and they chuckled together. "I suppose you get that in your ministry as well. People seeing that you write and speak for the Lord and assume that you don't struggle with selfishness and pride and any kind of sin, that you're perfect."

"I think that's a problem with ministry. There is that fine line. Where you need to be living the things that you preach, but you're still human, and you're never going to be perfect." She looked down. "I guess that was part of the reason that I put my daughter out of sight and out of mind. I didn't want to ruin the illusion of perfection. I worked hard at it. Not that I ever claimed to be perfect," she said quickly. "But people expected that for me. They wouldn't be very happy or supportive if they found out about the sin in my past."

"I think they would relate to you more. A lot of times, especially if you've grown from your mistake. If you can call it that. I mean, God takes our mistakes and makes something beautiful out of them. Dabney. I know that the night you spent with that guy was sin, but the fact that Dabney is here just underlines the fact that God could use your sin and make something beautiful out of it."

It still bothered him, the idea of her with someone else, but he shrugged it off. That was something he couldn't change. He couldn't do a single thing about it, and while he figured he would always have some jealousy in that area, he needed to push it aside.

"I suppose that's part of what I've been learning. That I don't have to be perfect. That maybe there are lessons I could share with people about mistakes I've made, what I've learned. But I also think that maybe my learning process isn't complete."

He held his breath. When she didn't say anything more, he prompted her, "What do you think you still need to learn?"

"I'm still thinking on it," she said, then she turned back toward the oven. "I think my next tray of cookies is done. You haven't tried them yet. How am I supposed to know if they're any good?"

"I can tell you they smell divine," he said as he picked up a cookie, disappointed she wouldn't continue to talk to him.

He bit into it, and he figured he should have known that if Mertie did it, it would be perfect, but it was definitely the best chocolate chip cookie he'd ever had, although he would never tell his mother that.

He had just swallowed when his phone started to ring.

Mertie looked over her shoulder. "Do you need me to leave?"

"No." He pulled his phone out, looking at it before he spoke to her. "It's Vera Miller. I hope everything's okay," he said as he put the phone to his ear. "Hello?"

"Garnet. I'm sorry to be bothering you on Sunday afternoon." Vera sounded like she was out of breath.

"It's okay."

"I just want to let you know that I'm at the hospital. Getting ready to have a C-section."

"Congratulations. Do you need help?"

"No. Actually, they won't let anyone except Dominic in, but I was supposed to meet with Norma Jean tomorrow morning for Bible study. I'm...not going to be able to make it, and I would cancel, but I think she really needs it. Maybe even her husband. I was hoping you could go."

"Sure. They live out on the road by the store?"

"Yeah. That road."

"What time?" he asked, hoping that she would be able to get it out, because it sounded like she was in distress. Obviously, if her twins were ready to arrive, she was probably excited, even in labor, he wasn't sure how that worked with a C-section.

"Nine o'clock tomorrow morning. Also, I'm looking for someone to watch our kids. I have Skyler doing it, but she already has Gertie and her own child, and... I don't know who to ask."

"I'll see what I can do," he said, knowing that a small-town pastor often did things like this, and even though he wasn't hired yet, he racked his brain to think of who might go and watch Vera's four small children that she was in the process of adopting with her husband.

"Does she need something?" Mertie asked softly, obviously hearing at least his side of the conversation.

"She needs someone to watch her children, the kids she's adopting, since she's having a C-section right now. You know of anyone in town who could do that?" He couldn't think of anyone. Maybe Amara could.

"I can do it. Does she need me to go now?"

He stared at her. Of course she could do it. Mertie could handle anything, even four small children, but he had wanted to spend the afternoon with her. Had wanted to get to know her, talk to her, convince her that she should stay in Raspberry Ridge and be a mom, and...be more than a friend to him. But if that wasn't what the Lord wanted for her, he didn't want her doing it.

There was some mumbling on the other end of the line. Possibly a doctor or Dominic talking to Vera. He didn't wait for her to say anything to him but said, "Mertie and I will go watch your kids."

"Perfect. Thank you so much. Mrs. Higginbotham can come this evening, but they were visiting friends this afternoon. It'll just be for a couple of hours."

"We'll be right there, so Skyler can go back to taking care of Gertie and her daughter."

"I'll have Dominic text her and let her know. I need to go. Thank you so much," Vera said.

Garnet swiped off his phone, holding it in his hand for a second before he said, "I told her we'd leave now."

"I heard you." Mertie was already bending over, taking the trays out of the oven. "These are going to be a little undercooked, but they're going to have to do. Actually, I'll box some of these up, and we'll take them for the kids."

"Good idea. I'll go tell Mom that we're going to be going out for a bit. Vera has someone coming this evening, but she said it will be a couple of hours."

"All right. We can handle it." She looked over her shoulder and gave him a confident smile. There was no doubt in his mind that Mertie could handle it. She had a rock-solid confidence that just exuded from everything she did and made him feel confident at the same time. All he had to do was look at her and know that God was in control. He never met anyone else who pointed him to the Lord so clearly and effortlessly.

Nineteen

"I had fun," Dabney said as she practically skipped along beside Mertie.

"I'm glad Mertie thought to ask you if you wanted to come. I'm not sure I would have," Garnet said, meeting Mertie's eyes over the top of Dabney's head.

Dabney was just a couple of inches shorter than Mertie and almost certainly would be taller than her once she was done growing.

Mertie smiled, thinking that inviting Dabney to come help watch the children had been a stroke of brilliance on her part, although it had just been a last-minute thought as they were walking out the door.

But Dabney had obviously loved working with the children, and after seeing them in church, she was familiar with their names and had been a big help.

Mrs. Higginbotham had come several hours later than what they were expecting, but it hadn't mattered at all. They'd all been enjoying themselves, and Mertie thought that it had bonded them together in a way that recreation couldn't. When people were doing a job, a job that had meaning and that they believed in, when they were pulling together for the same goal, keeping kids alive, that had been Mertie's goal anyway, it did seem to bond them. And that's what she needed with Dabney, something that bonded her to the girl.

"I hope it was okay that when I texted Vera and told her that Mrs. Higginbotham was there and was taking over, Dominic asked me if we would be interested in watching the children any other time this week. I... I might have said yes."

Mertie laughed.

"Yay! You mean we're going back?" Dabney said as she took a couple of skipping steps, acting like she was truly happy. Some people really were good with children, had a natural affinity for them, and really loved them. Dabney seemed like that type of person, and Mertie figured she got it from her dad. Although... Mertie hadn't hated this evening. She'd done better than she expected. She always thought that she was the kind of person who related better to adults, but watching the kids had been fun.

Maybe it was because she was doing it with Garnet and Dabney.

"I told him I thought we could, but I needed to talk to the two of you first."

"I'll do it!" Dabney said, then she looked at Mertie. Mertie couldn't have said no if her life depended on it.

"I'd love to." She found those words were absolutely true. Even though she wouldn't be spending one-on-one time with Garnet, and taking care of four kids was not exactly a walk in the park, it was a ministry. Not the kind of ministry that she was used to, but the kind of servant ministry that Jesus called Christians to.

There were no accolades, and no one saw her. It wasn't a bit like her speaking ministry where she had the rapt attention of hundreds of adults in the room, or her book ministry where hundreds of thousands if not millions of people were reached. This was small, unknown, unloved, and mostly unappreciated, but it was perfect. God knew what she needed was not more accolades, but a purpose, a ministry that she could do with her daughter, and...Garnet. Whatever he was to her. Her friend?

"I'll go ahead and text Dominic. Are there any times that don't suit you? Just in case he asks."

"I should be able to do it anytime. I'm off, all I have to do is help get the house ready, but we're doing what we can until Olive comes, so there's no pressure there."

Maybe the Lord had ordained that too. Funny how things were working out. Of course, she should know by now that God always worked things out. She'd seen it time and time again.

"Do you work with kids in your regular job?" Dabney asked as they walked along, Garnet working on tapping the message on his phone.

"I actually don't. I hardly ever work with children. This was a new and eye-opening experience." She decided she could be honest. "I wasn't sure I was going to like them."

"It seemed like you had a good time. While we were playing hide-and-seek, you were laughing as much as anyone."

"I think your dad and you have the edge on that, because I'm pretty sure you guys have played hide-and-seek before together."

"It was my favorite game growing up. And Dad always played with me. I didn't realize it when I was little, but the older I get, the more I realize he's pretty awesome."

It seemed like a wise statement for a 14-year-old, but Garnet had said she was mature for her age.

"I can see why it was your favorite game. I've actually never played it before, but I enjoyed it."

"You never played it when you were a kid?" She sounded aghast.

"No. Not even when I was a kid. We didn't really play games at my house. Particularly after my parents started a business together. They were busy."

"Dad works hard, but he always has time for me. When I talked to my friends about it, they admitted they have dads who don't really spend much time with them at all. I felt bad for them, but it made me realize how good Dad is."

"He kind of has to be mom and dad for you, doesn't he?" Mertie said, and she hoped she wasn't skating too close to what she really wanted to talk about, which was Dabney and how she felt about having a mom.

"He tries. I don't want to say it too often, especially as I've gotten older, how much I wish I had a mom, because I know Dad has done the best he can." She looked over her shoulder at Garnet, who was following a couple of steps behind, since his phone had rung and he had answered it, and it sounded like he was talking to Dominic. It sounded like the twins had been born and they were healthy. But Mertie was mostly focusing on the girl in front of her. Her daughter.

"That's very thoughtful of you. I don't think that most children your age are quite that thoughtful."

"Well, for a long time it was just Daddy and me. I heard my homeschool teachers sometimes say that when kids spend a lot of time with adults, they have a tendency to mature more quickly, because that's their role model. When they spend a lot of time with other kids in the classroom, they all kind of hold each other back, because they imitate their peers rather than the adults because that's who they spend their time with."

Her daughter sounded so intelligent. But she was probably absolutely right, although Mertie had never really thought about it.

"I'm glad your dad homeschooled you."

"I'm glad he did too. I don't think he really did it because he wanted to, but I think he did it because he was afraid of the things I might learn if he sent me to school."

"There are a lot of schools and teachers who are really good," Mertie started. "But the chance that you might get someone who's not gets bigger and bigger every year."

"I think Dad said something to that effect, but I just know I would rather be with Dad than be in a whole classroom full of kids who aren't interested in learning, with a teacher who wants to teach me things that aren't true."

"The twins were born, and they're healthy." Garnet took a couple running steps to catch back up with them. "Dominic sounds like a proud father, although I think he's a little overwhelmed. They have six children now, and he couldn't quite get over that."

"They'll be a little crazy," Mertie said, heartfelt. She couldn't imagine having six kids. Couldn't begin to imagine. She felt a little overwhelmed sometimes when she remembered that she had a daughter who was fourteen. What if she had six kids she had to get to know?

She shivered at the thought.

"That would be awesome. To be in a family of six kids. I wish that were our family." Dabney spoke softly, almost as though she knew her words might upset her dad, but she couldn't keep from saying them.

"You want siblings?" Mertie asked, hearing the longing in her voice.

"Oh, I do. So much. Dad is awesome." She beamed up a smile at Garnet, who returned it, but it wasn't hard to see the consternation on his face that he hadn't been able to give his daughter the things she most wanted. "But I wouldn't want to have a whole bunch of siblings who didn't have a mom. It stinks."

One more thing Garnet couldn't give her, but Mertie could.

Of course, Garnet could get married, but he wouldn't want just anyone to be Dabney's mother. He would be particular. Careful. And if Dabney wasn't interested, Garnet would walk away.

Mertie was sure of that with her whole heart.

"You know, sometimes God has a way of giving us the things that we most want." Mertie heard the words coming out of her mouth, but she wasn't quite sure why she was saying them. It wasn't like she was going to do anything to change the situation. At least not with siblings. Except... She wasn't too old to have children.

They made it down to the main street of Raspberry Ridge and turned right up the street, heading toward Garnet's parents' house.

No one said anything much, and when they got to the house, Dabney hurried in, calling out to her gram and starting into a story about what they had done.

Garnet had stopped on the porch, and Mertie stopped with him.

"Can I walk you home?" he asked softly.

She hadn't even thought about that. She should have walked to her own house instead of walking to his, but the conversation with Dabney had been so interesting, the evening so perfect, she hadn't even thought about going home.

"Your parents and your daughter might need you." She didn't want to take him away from his responsibilities.

"I'll let them know where I'm going. It won't take long."

He was right about that, so she waited on the porch while he called in that he was going to walk her home, and then the door closed softly behind him as his hand slipped into hers, and they walked off the porch together.

She wanted to make a comment that he was holding her hand now but hadn't done it in front of Dabney, but she didn't know what it meant and didn't know whether it was something that he would be sensitive about. She didn't want to tease him about anything that might make him self-conscious or feel bad. That wasn't her goal in life.

"I had such a good time tonight, and I think you can see that Dabney did too."

"Yeah. And I think you saw that I did as well."

"I thought you were, but I wasn't sure if that was your happy face or if that was you truly having a good time."

"That was me truly having a good time."

"I'm happy to hear it."

"Are we still on for tomorrow?" she asked, knowing that she needed to get to bed, because they had to be at Norma Jean's house at nine o'clock the next morning. It was going to be a short night. And she needed to talk to her sister, to let her know what was going on. She hadn't talked to her since Amara had left church without her.

"Is that going to be too much for you? I can do it if you don't want to."

"It's kind of my thing. I'm happy to help, if I can."

"I don't know if her husband will be there, but I thought you might be able to handle Norma Jean, Dabney might be able to watch her daughter, Holly, and I could talk to her husband, Miles. We'd be killing three birds with...three stones, I guess."

"One visit. That can be one stone."

"There you go. The three of us can just do a multidirectional attack."

"We're in a battle, I suppose."

"We sure are." His voice trailed off, as though that was something that weighed on his mind. As a pastor, called to preach God's word, she would assume that that probably was something that he thought about quite often.

They walked a few more steps in the dark, their hands linked between them, and she was tempted to ask him what exactly that meant, but she was afraid she didn't want to know, or maybe wasn't ready for, the answer.

"Have you thought about whether or not you want Dabney to know that you're her mother? And how it might look when you tell her?"

His words came out on the air and landed heavy and hard on her ears. Even though he said them gently. She just...knew she needed to, but... "I haven't thought about it at all."

"Okay." There was disappointment in his tone.

"Telling her. I haven't thought about telling her. All I can think about is being her mom and what a great dad you are. You were on the phone, but she was telling me how awesome you were, how she knew from the other kids she talked to that having a dad like you was unusual."

"Really?" he asked, surprise and hope in his tone.

"Yeah. It's kind of a mature sentiment from a fourteen-year-old. They're supposed to be rebelling against their parents, not talking about how wonderful they are, but she is mature for her age."

"It's because we—"

"Homeschool." She laughed. "Dabney told me all about how superior homeschooling is to other forms of schooling."

"Sorry."

"It's okay. I wasn't offended, I just know there are good teachers, but also homeschool is probably best. I don't know that I could have done it though. I admire you."

"I couldn't have done it, except God helped. That's pretty much the story of my life. God did it, and I just kind of held on and did my best."

That was the best kind of life. It truly was. A life that was completely surrendered to the Lord, where He guided it, and she would just work as hard as she could at whatever He put in front of her. Whether that was speaking engagements in front of hundreds of people or babysitting for adopted children while their mother had twins at the hospital.

"Thank you for tonight."

"I think that might be the first time in the history of the world that anyone has ever thanked anyone else for dragging them along to babysit four children."

"I meant it. I enjoyed spending time with you and Dabney. You have a bond, and it's special. I'm not sure I would fit in."

"You would."

"Are you trying to convince yourself or me?"

"We can ask Dabney."

She had a feeling he might be right about that. She might see that she would fit in.

"You just have a way about you. Just... You belong in our family. I don't think Dabney could miss it if she tried. I certainly haven't."

"I don't want to upset anything. She obviously loves and respects you very much. And you love and respect her. Bringing a third person in could upset things."

"You could end up having more children."

She stopped abruptly, almost choking on her saliva as his words seemed to ring out in the night air. "You're not talking about just visiting occasionally."

"Did you misunderstand what I've been saying?"

She didn't say anything. She had really misunderstood.

He held up their joined hands. "This isn't something I do with my friends."

She felt faint. Her breath came fast.

"You don't have to make a decision right now. I'm not pressuring you for anything. But I wasn't really thinking about visits. I was thinking about...how back when we were friends, it was never quite enough for me, but we were young, and I didn't really think about doing more until after you left. Then when you came back with your baby, I was...jealous. But you didn't have to ask me twice."

"You took her right away. Never questioned anything. I felt like you didn't mind at all. Although, at the time I really did think you were putting her up for adoption."

"I did."

"You know what I mean."

"Yeah. It's okay if you don't feel it. I just know where I stand."

"I didn't say I didn't feel anything." She couldn't say more. She couldn't explain what she felt. She wasn't even sure she knew.

They had reached the bottom of the steps that went up to her house, and she hesitated for just a moment before pulling her hand from his.

"I can make it from here. Thank you. I'll see you in the morning."

She didn't wait for him to answer before she turned and started walking up the steps. She wasn't desperate to get away from him, she was just desperate to think, to figure it out. She hated it when things felt like they weren't in her control. She wanted her life to be well ordered, where she knew exactly what was happening, how she felt about it, what she was going to do. None of it felt like it was in her control right now.

"Good night, Mertie."

She closed her eyes, slowing but not stopping. His words sent shivers down her spine, and she wanted to stop, turn around, run to him. Was that what she was supposed to do? Because if it was, there was no way she could say yes to Zebedee Clinger. Sure, she could work, but she didn't want to do that when she was married. She'd heard too many Christian marriages breaking apart because one of the partners got a little too chummy with the person they were working with. She didn't want that to be her. Plus, if she got married, she wanted to be a wife, a mother, and if Garnet got the pastorate, she would be a pastor's wife, someone who helped out in the church, stood beside her husband, did what she could to be a helper to him.

She didn't want to spend days away from her family, speaking and doing all the things that she would need to do, somewhere other than Raspberry Ridge. She just couldn't reconcile the two.

She took two more slow steps before she said, "Good night, Garnet."

Twenty

Miles stood beside the barn and watched the car pull into the drive.

According to Norma Jean, the new pastor and some woman were supposed to be coming to do the Bible study Miss Vera normally did.

Miles shoved a hand in his pocket and wished his disappointment was just as easy to shove down.

His wife had actually been acting more like a wife - relative - since Vera had started doing her Bible study. Miles had hope that their marriage might survive after all.

But, with Vera off having twins, he didn't hold too much hope that these two were going to continue down the same path. Vera had been teaching his wife actual Biblical precepts. Not some modern mumbo jumbo that encouraged her to live her truth or worry about her self-esteem, or want him to be a pansy.

He wouldn't have proposed a marriage of convenience with Norma Jean if he hadn't thought they could eventually make a go of it, but he hadn't expected it to be so hard. Originally he wanted a mom for his daughter, and Norma had her own ulterior motives.

Of course, if he'd known that those motives were to make another man jealous, he might have been a little less eager to shackle himself to her.

He straightened as the man, who had been chatting with Norma Jean in the doorway of their house, turned and headed toward the barn where Miles stood, while the woman walked into the house.

So...maybe it wasn't the new pastor, or almost-pastor, after all. They hadn't made it to church on Sunday and he didn't know what the man looked like.

This dude looked a little too rugged, too...not like a preacher to be a preacher.

Miles pushed off the post where he'd been leaning just inside the barn doorway. Too late to try to make it look like he'd been working.

"You must be Miles," the man said as he entered the barn with his hand out, a friendly smile on his face.

He gave Miles the feeling that he could be trusted. He wasn't sure what it was about the man that made him feel like he was already a friend, before Miles had even said a word. He took the proffered hand and shook it.

"Yep, that's me. You're the new pastor?" He took a guess.

"Not yet. I still have another sermon to give, then the congregation will vote on me. That's this coming Sunday."

The guy didn't look nervous or anxious. It was like he didn't care whether he was voted in or not.

Didn't care...or had faith that God was going to work everything out. Miles figured it was the latter. He liked a pastor who lived what he preached. His opinion of the man, already abnormally high for a stranger, just went up a few more notches.

"I met a lot of people in church on Sunday. Forgive me for not remembering you."

"I wasn't there." He didn't elaborate. There was no reason or excuse. He...just hadn't felt that close to the Lord in recent weeks.

"My...friend, Mertie Jerdine, is inside chatting with your wife."

"It was my understanding that you were going to take Vera's place in her weekly Bible study."

"Well," the man ran a hand over his head. "That was the idea. Only,

Mertie has her own ministry as a Christian speaker and author and I figured she was more equipped than I to speak to Norma Jean, so I asked her to do it while I came out here to see if you'd be interested in a little manly study."

Miles almost sighed out loud. He didn't really want to do a study with the new pastor, but his work was not pressing and a little voice told him that maybe he shouldn't be placing the entire burden of their marriage on Norma Jean. Just because he felt a little angry - make that hurt and betrayed because she'd married him to make another man jealous, even if it was supposed to be a marriage of convenience.

"Sure. My physical Bible is in the house, but I have one downloaded on my phone."

"That'll work." Garnet looked indescribably pleased.

"We could sit over there," Miles said, nodding toward a few hay bales on the sunny side of the barn. It wasn't so hot that they needed shade, and he'd rather be on the side of the barn away from the house. For some reason, he didn't want Norma Jean to look out and see him sitting with the pastor. He wasn't sure why and didn't question it.

They walked around the side of the barn, the smell of freshly made hay filling the air with its down home goodness. He'd never get tired of the scents of the farm. They reminded him of home and made him feel good the whole way to his soul.

When Norma Jean had suggested they sell the farm and move to town, he'd almost told her she could leave and good riddance. Not that he hated her, but after she admitted that she'd been trying to impress another man, married him out of spite and to induce jealousy and then she didn't even love the home of his heart like she'd pretended to...yeah. He still found her attractive, but wasn't sure he'd not made the biggest mistake of his life by marrying her.

The pastor settled himself and prayed, while Miles wondered if he was going to get dismissed before noon. He hadn't thought that the man was going to keep him for hours, but he seemed to be settling in like it was going to be a while.

"Is there any part of your marriage that you'd like to talk about? Not to pry, but I figured I'd ask first, before I started in with something that might not be as helpful or relevant to any issues you're having."

"No." Miles knew his word was short, but even though he liked the man right away, he didn't want to talk about his marriage with him.

Why not?

The little voice was soft, but insistent in his head.

Why not, indeed. If his wife was taking the time to meet with ladies who were trying to help her, he could put forth the same kind of effort, couldn't he?

He thought of Holly, his daughter who had already lost her mother. She deserved his best effort. She had warmed to Norma Jean and a divorce would rip apart her world.

"Sometimes I resent my wife."

The pastor's brows went up, but he didn't look shocked. Rather, he seemed thoughtful.

"Why?"

"She lied when she married me." He didn't put the hurt in his heart in those words. They seemed kind of cold, even though that was the farthest thing from what he felt.

"Oh."

He thought he would have to explain what the lie was and all of that, but, to his surprise, the pastor didn't ask. Rather he said, "Have you ever lied?"

"I have," he said. "But I couldn't tell you the last time."

"I see. Do you want God to forgive you for your lies?"

"Of course." That was common sense.

"If you want God to forgive you, shouldn't you forgive your wife?"

Miles stared at the pastor, thoughtful. He knew he needed to forgive his wife. But, "Don't you want to know what she lied about?"

"It doesn't matter."

"But it has to do with why she married me."

"You're married now. How you got that way doesn't matter." The pastor twirled the haystem he held in his hand. "You can't hold on to the past."

"But she might do it again."

"She might. Have you ever sinned twice with the same thing?"

"Of course." There were a few sins he struggled with on a daily, sometimes, hourly, basis.

"Does God give you a hard time because you did it again? Does He refuse to forgive you because He's afraid that since you did it twice, you might do it a third time?"

Miles took a breath. It was more like since he'd done it ten thousand times, and he might do it ten thousand one.

"No." He didn't want to speak the truth, but any other answer would be a lie.

"Forgiveness is hard, I know. But your responsibility as a husband is to love your wife, provide for her, and know her as best you can, giving yourself for her as Christ gave himself for the church. It doesn't really matter what she does."

What? It didn't matter what his wife did?

Maybe the pastor saw the look on his face. "What? Did I say something you can refute with a Bible verse?"

Oh, boy. Of course he could. But as he sat there thinking, he realized that, no, he couldn't think of a single verse that said that his wife had to ask for forgiveness and be remorseful and start to love him before he did what he had been commanded to do. Ouch.

"I know. It's hard. Believe me, I looked for an out for a long time after I first heard that. I grew up hearing that marriage is a partnership and each partner has to do the work and it's 50-50 or 100-100, but the basic idea was that what you do depends on what she does, and if she doesn't do what she's supposed to, then you don't have to stay with her, because how can you be "happy" with someone who doesn't try to be a good wife?"

The whole thing was just...absurd. Miles couldn't figure out what was so wrong about it, but he knew that something was. It couldn't be true that his marriage was all his responsibility.

"Doesn't she have to do anything?" he asked, trying not to sound desperate and angry.

"She has her own commands from the Lord, ones she has to obey, whether or not you obey yours, but it's not your job to hold her to them, regulate her, or make sure she is doing what she's supposed to. It's your job to do you. To love her, to protect and provide for her, to know her, as well as a man can know a woman, and to give yourself for her as Christ gave himself for the church. He gave himself for the church long before anyone started to follow Him or love Him. It was His example, after all, that drew us to Him."

Everything the pastor said made sense. He couldn't argue, although he wanted to. He huffed out a breath. "You don't mess around with bottle feeding. You just throw big hunks of meat at people."

The pastor laughed at his half-hearted attempt to paraphrase the Bible. But he was serious. Pastor Garnet had just given him a huge chunk to chew on.

"Alright, I didn't want to keep you from your work. Is there something I can help you with until the ladies are done?"

And just like that, they stood up from the bales and the new almost-pastor started tossing fifty pound seed bags from the pallet where they'd been sitting to the back corner of the barn where he wanted to store them for winter.

The guy wasn't half bad, and, while he wasn't sure about what he'd said, he was going to check out his Bible and see if he could find somewhere it contradicted everything the pastor had laid out. He hoped so, but somehow he doubted it.

"Are you nervous?"

Mertie glanced at Garnet, who looked as cool as a person could. But everything he had planned hinged on this sermon being a smashing success.

"Not really. I'm comfortable speaking in front of people, and I know what I'm going to say. I hope I can give God the credit He deserves, but otherwise, I'm excited."

He looked like he meant every word.

Dabney had gone ahead of them to meet a couple of kids from her class, and there were people milling about in the parking lot. Soon Garnet would be chatting and she would need to step back and allow him to do his job, pastor the people of this church.

And he seemed ready for it. She could only wish she had his faith. That must be why he wasn't nervous. Whatever happened was in God's hands.

She could learn a few things from him.

"So, in another couple of hours you could be the new pastor."

"Actually, no."

"What?" She almost shouted it, but lowered her voice just in time. "What are you talking about?"

"The Bible says that a pastor is the husband of one wife. I'm not the husband of any. I told the Lord when I applied for this position that if He didn't provide a wife, I wasn't going to accept it. Now, God sometimes cuts things pretty close, and I wanted to give Him all the time He wanted, just having faith that everything would work out, but, the fact of the matter is, I'm not going to be a permanent pastor if I don't have a wife."

"Oh."

Of course. That made total sense to her. She knew the passage he spoke of, although she'd never applied it like that. She just assumed a pastor couldn't be divorced and remarried. It hadn't occurred to her that he needed to be married to begin with.

Mrs. Brandstetter headed their way, and she moved back so Garnet could speak with her. Looking around, she was disappointed to not see Becky, whom she'd spoken with the last Sunday. She'd been praying for her, just having the feeling that God was working on her about something and wanting to help if she could.

It ended up that Garnet had another amazing sermon. She couldn't explain why she felt so proud of him. It wasn't like she had anything to do with it, but her heart just swelled as he spoke the last words and the congregation bowed their heads for the altar call.

She couldn't wait to tell him how amazing his sermon was, but that joy and excitement was tempered by the idea that no matter how good it was, he wasn't going to be the pastor here.

Unless he had a wife.

The words stopped her cold. She didn't want Garnet to have a wife. *Not unless it was her.*

She blinked. Where did that thought come from? She wasn't interested in getting married, wanted to finish up cleaning up the house so she could accept Zebedee's offer and move on with her own career, except...was that really what she wanted?

Dominic Miller stood up as the congregation sat down. He thanked Garnet. "If you'd like to go somewhere, we'll call you when the results are in. We're going to have a chance for everyone to chat a bit, so plan on an hour or so."

Garnet shook his hand, nodded and walked off the platform. Since

Mertie wasn't a member of the church, she wouldn't be voting, so as Garnet walked by, she tapped Dabney's arm and they both stood up and followed him out.

They could hear Dominic talking as they closed the door behind them.

"I think everyone liked it, Dad. At least no one was sleeping that I could see."

Mertie bit back a laugh at Dabney's definition of a good sermon - it kept everyone awake. She supposed that maybe wasn't a terrible litmus test.

"I thought it was excellent as well. Truly fantastic." She didn't know how to tell him that his message on seeking the Lord and accepting His will for their life had hit closer to home than she wanted to admit. After all, she only really wanted to do God's will when it was her will too. And she wanted her will to be God's will.

As Garnet had said, it was often easy to tell what was the Lord's will because it wouldn't be the easy way and was often not the way they, or the rest of the world, thought they should do things.

"Thanks." Garnet looked pleased. "I'm happy my two favorite ladies enjoyed my sermon." He put an arm around Dabney and an arm around Mertie and squeezed. She allowed herself to be pulled closer and enjoyed standing beside him. A longing deep in her soul to make this her family surprised her with its strength. Much stronger than any longing to have a brilliant career.

Garnet squeezed one more time, then let go. "What do you say we walk home and check on Gram and Pap?"

"Dad?" Dabney said, her voice muffled like she was still pressed against his side.

"Yeah, Sweetie?"

"When are you and Miss Mertie going to tell me that Miss Mertie is my mom?"

Mertie froze. So did Garnet, and both of them were absolutely quiet.

"Where did you hear that?" he said, his voice just above a whisper.

"Does it matter?" Mertie asked, pulling away from him and moving so she could see both her daughter and her daughter's dad.

"No. I guess it doesn't."

"Gram told me. She said Mrs. Calvin's sister, the nurse who delivered me, told her when she visited Mrs. Calvin to deliver cookies." Dabney looked down for a moment, as though thinking. Mertie was too stunned to say anything, and perhaps that was Garnet's issue, too, since neither of them spoke.

Finally, Garnet asked, "How long have you known?"

Dabney shuffled her feet and pursed her lips, still looking at the ground. Finally, she glanced up.

"You know the first day we saw her? At the Bible study?"

Mertie swallowed hard. She'd practically run from that Bible study. What must Dabney think? She didn't want her daughter to think she didn't want her.

"Yes?" Garnet said, compassion in his voice. "You knew then?"

"Not really. Not at first. But," Dabney paused for a moment. "She looks like me. I mean, it's not exactly like looking in a mirror. But, all my life, I've looked at people and tried to see myself in them." She lifted a shoulder. "I don't want you to think that you're not a good dad, or that I'm not happy with you. That's probably why I never said anything. And when we talk about it, I always say the bad things about the ladies we are looking at, but with Miss Mertie...she looked like me. Like, my eyes, like a shadow of the reflection I see every day. And, I tried to ask you about her, but I just couldn't come right out and ask. I thought you'd tell me."

Garnet's lips pressed together and Mertie could almost feel his pain, thinking about his daughter wondering about her mother and him never knowing.

"So, anyway, I just wondered if you guys are ever going to tell me. Gram said to give you time, but I have. At least it seems like I've waited a long time"

She twisted her hands in front of her. "I know you said that you weren't going to take the pastorate here if God didn't send you a wife, and I kept waiting for you and Mertie to announce that you're together, but you don't even seem to be trying."

Dabney's voice gradually got louder until she was practically shrieking.

Mertie's eyes fluttered, and, while her head spun with thoughts of the offer from Zebedee and her career, her heart felt quiet and at peace.

Who else had supported her, stood with her - even if they weren't together - and always made decisions that were best for her? Garnet had been a friend to her, even when she hadn't realized it, and sometimes when she hadn't wanted it. He'd never wavered in his steadfast support.

"Do you mind if I talk to your...mother alone?" Garnet asked softly.

"So, she really is my mother?"

"I am." Mertie cut in, taking a step and reaching a hand out to touch Dabney's arm. She didn't pull away. "I am, and I have so much to talk to you about, but the most important thing I want to make sure you know is that I loved you so much and wanted the very best for you. I didn't think I could give that to you."

When her hand touched Dabney's arm, Dabney looked up, and as tears filled her eyes, Dabney moved closer before throwing her arms around her.

"That's what Dad always said." She squeezed tight and held her for long moments. But then she pulled away, wiping a cheek. "We can talk later?"

"This afternoon. As soon as I talk to your dad."

"He loves you. I could always tell that he did. No one else ever caught his eye."

Dabney looked at her dad for his approval. Mertie noticed his cheeks had reddened, but he nodded.

"Let me talk to her." He ruffled Dabney's hair, and she laughed and pulled away, turning to continue down the sidewalk without them.

Mertie waited for her to walk out of earshot before she asked, "Is that true?"

His gaze shot to hers and his eyes widened. But he didn't ask what she was talking about.

He shifted, shoving his hand in his pocket as his jaw muscle twitched in and out.

"Yes. It's true."

$$Twenty-Two$$

Garnet forced himself to meet Mertie's eyes. She deserved the truth.

"Why didn't you mention that you weren't going to take the pastorate unless God gave you a wife?"

That wasn't the question he expected from her. He'd expected her to grill him on the fact that his daughter had just told her that he loved her and he'd admitted it was true.

But Mertie often didn't do the expected thing. He knew her well enough to know that.

"I told the Lord I was leaving it in His hands. I'm hardly leaving things in His hands if I'm worrying about it constantly. I honestly tried not to think about it. You know, I could count down the days: *Lord, you only have a week to drop that wife in my lap.* And in my human thinking, I wouldn't be able to figure out how I could find a woman to agree to be my wife in three weeks, two weeks, one week, five days, three hours..." His voice trailed off. He'd had those thoughts. Mostly at night as he was falling asleep. But he always pushed them aside. They were not helpful in any way.

Her lips pulled back and she looked away.

"What?" It seemed like she wasn't happy with his answer.

She fiddled with a loose piece of her shirt, biting her lip.

"If you love me, like Dabney says, why wouldn't you ask me?" She pulled in a breath. "I mean, doesn't it seem like God has just dropped me here and that's what He intended?"

"You have a career. You mentioned the opportunity you've been offered. A once in a lifetime deal, and you might not have said, but a husband and daughter would hardly help, and in fact, might keep you from reaching for what you really want."

"Maybe you should ask me what I really want?" She lifted her brows and looked like the woman who had arrived in Raspberry Ridge, serene and untouchable.

But he knew the Mertie he'd been friends with...had loved....for years was just under the surface. That cool exterior was just a ruse.

"Mertie? What do you want?"

"I want to be a mother to my daughter. To be a mother to as many children as the Lord gives me. To get married. To you. My best friend."

His head tilted. He wanted to point out that he hadn't asked her to marry him.

"Garnet? Will you marry me?"

He laughed. He'd never even kissed her. Not that he didn't want to. Not that it mattered. It was what he wanted since she'd brought her daughter and dropped her off with him - for them to be a family together.

"Yes." He took a step closer, putting his arms around her and drawing her close. "I will. If you're sure?" It was his dream, but he didn't want her to have to give up her dream in order for him to have what he wanted.

"I'm sure. God could not have been more clear. But, beyond that, I realized today that I love you. Maybe I have for a long time. Why else would I give you the most precious thing in the world to me? I trusted you more than I've ever trusted anyone."

"I've loved you forever. Even back when we were kids, although I didn't realize it." He put his hand on the back of her neck under her hair and felt her shiver.

She smiled up at him and he stared into her eyes before he lowered his head, kissing his best friend and the woman he loved.

He wasn't nearly done kissing her when he realized that someone was calling his name.

Pulling his head back reluctantly, he blinked a few times to orient himself and figure out what the person wanted.

"Pastor Garnet?"

It was Dominic.

"Uh," He cleared his throat. "Yeah? I mean, yes?"

"You weren't answering your phone, so I came out to look for you."

"Oh. I had my phone on silent for the service."

Mertie had pulled away just a bit, but he kept his arm around her.

"It looks like the church will be getting a pastor, his daughter and a wife. The decision was unanimous, but I'm sure this will be good news for everyone."

"For me, too." Garnet smiled.

"Do you want to come say a few words to the congregation?"

"I'd love to, but I need to call my daughter first. She deserves to be there."

"Of course. I'll let everyone know. We'll be waiting." Dominic turned and walked back toward the church.

"Why would he think we're getting married just because we're kissing?" Mertie wondered as he pulled his phone out of his pocket.

"I told him that I had made a vow that I wouldn't kiss anyone I wasn't planning on marrying. It just seems foolish and awkward in a weird way to kiss someone I have no intention of spending the rest of my life with. She might not be someone else's wife now, but she will be." He lifted a shoulder. It wasn't something that the rest of the world understood, and he knew that. It also wasn't expressly forbidden by scripture, but it seemed like a good standard to have. One Jesus would have if He were dating. He couldn't imagine Jesus just going around kissing anyone. The thought was repulsive.

"I can't tell you how many times you've inspired me to think harder, deeper and to look at my life and make changes."

He hugged her. "I think that's a good thing?"

"Most definitely a good thing." She smiled. "We're going to have to talk about a wedding."

"It's enough that we've agreed to it for me to take the pastorate." He could ask the committee to wait to officially hire him until after they were married, even if it took months. They'd figure it out.

"And I need to talk to Dabney."

"That is music to my ears. It seemed to me that she was okay, happy, even thrilled that you would be her mom."

"I just feel terrible that she's been without one for so long."

"She knows you did what you thought was best. That's all you can do. But, she has a mom for the rest of your life."

"And siblings."

He froze.

"You don't want more children?"

"I hadn't thought about it. Definitely. Siblings for Dabney, and another little girl with your eyes."

"And your smile and wisdom."

He couldn't help it. He leaned down and kissed her again. His congregation was going to have to wait.

Epilogue

Olive Jardine parked her car in the church lot and sat with her hands on the steering wheel. It was Sunday afternoon and it seemed liked the entire town was still at the church. If that was how long the sermons were going to last, she wasn't going to attend this church.

But she knew she needed to get back to the Lord. She'd strayed too far for too long.

She'd planned to come, to sit in the cool, quiet sanctuary and pray. Something she hadn't done for more years than she cared to admit.

Other than the desperate pleas she'd made the last few weeks. Pleas for her survival and her recovery. For her child.

She looked in the rearview mirror at the child in the car seat behind her. Having a child had not been in her plan.

But she was tired of running around. Tired of running away. And after almost dying, she wanted nothing more to come somewhere she felt safe, if not loved. Which was why she found herself and her sleeping baby back here in Raspberry Ridge, sitting in front of the church.

She'd put off going "home," to the house she still shared with her sisters and the one they were supposed to be cleaning out and getting ready to sell. Mostly because she hadn't been completely truthful with her sisters, but also because the idea of selling the house seemed to rip the little bit of security she had completely away.

Not wanting to face an entire crowd of people, she figured that it might be best if she just ripped the bandage off with one quick pull, so to speak. So, she turned her borrowed car off, got the car seat out and walked toward the church, opening the door and standing in the back.

Her sister Mertie stood at the front, perfectly put together as always, a young girl on one side, and it looked like her childhood friend, Garnet Irving stood with her. Were they married? Was that their child?

She was ashamed to admit that she'd been so out of touch with her family that she really didn't know what was going on, although as far as she knew, Mertie had a Christian ministry that did not include a husband or a child.

Her eyes swept the room, looking for her other sister, Amara, but not finding her right away. Mostly because her eyes were caught on a tall figure, head and shoulders above everyone else, broad shoulders and that bright red hair that was unmistakable.

Doyle.

Just the sight of him made her want to turn around and run away, although she still felt the same pull that she always had, too. But her days of running were over. She had to remind herself of that as she fought to keep her feet planted on the floor. She would face whatever needed to be faced and deal with it, even if it was hard. She didn't want her daughter to see her cowardly example and emulate it.

As though pulled by her stare, Doyle tilted his head, then slowly turned, his gaze meeting hers almost immediately. It took two seconds before his eyes widened and the shock of recognition stole over his face. It took one more before he turned to the person beside him, leaned down and whispered something. They moved and he slipped out of the pew, as the man at the pulpit continued to speak.

The urge to run became almost uncontrollable as Olive watched the man she'd left eight years ago walk back the side aisle toward her.

She had a lot of explaining to do. That's if he was coming back to talk and not to strangle her. And that's if he was still talking to her after she told him about her child.

A lot of ifs.

But, if she wanted a life for her child in Raspberry Ridge, she was going to have to face them, answer them and deal with the consequences.

Lord, I need you.

She whispered those words as she turned to face the good man she'd hurt and betrayed.

Join Jessie's list and be the first to know about new releases and sales on her books!

<u>Read Into the Golden Dawn</u>, the next book in the Raspberry Ridge series where Olive Jardine joins her sister and the secret she's been keeping for more than a year is with her. When she's hired as Doyle Lowry's housekeeper, will she be able to keep from crushing on her boss? Keep reading for a sneak peek now.

Sneak Peek of Into the
Golden Dawn

This was not the time or place.

Olive Jardine stared at the man walking toward her, knowing she had a lot of explaining to do, and even more apologizing, but she stood at the back of the church in the middle of a church service, although it was well after noon on Sunday in Raspberry Ridge, Michigan. The town she'd grown up in. The town she'd spent her childhood in, although her parents had moved away before she graduated from high school.

Doyle McKenny, the man who had almost reached her side, was part of the reason she hadn't been back in years.

"Olive? Is that you?"

Olive swallowed hard. There was amazement on his face, but there was also a hint of the hurt that she'd inflicted, and once he knew for sure that it was her, she was sure that part of his expression would balloon into something she could hardly stand. Perhaps there would also be hate.

She glanced around the church. A couple of heads had turned when Doyle got up, but Olive's sister, Mertie, and some man Olive was pretty sure was Mertie's best friend from childhood, stood in front of the microphone, speaking, and most people were hanging on their every word.

Olive hadn't taken the time to try to figure out what they were saying. She'd been too shocked when she'd stepped in and seen the back of Doyle's head. It was unmistakable, since he was taller than everyone in the sanctuary, and if that wasn't enough to set him apart, he had hair the color of carrots.

Back in their childhood, when she had described his hair that way, he had always laughed. It hadn't bothered him a bit, even though originally Olive had said it as an insult, since Anne, from Anne of Green Gables, had been so upset about the comparison.

Men were different. At least Doyle was different.

She hadn't realized how different, maybe special was a better word, until she had travelled the world a little. It hadn't taken her long to realize that what she had left behind in Raspberry Ridge, thinking that there was something better out there, had been the best.

It amazed her sometimes that God had started her out with the very best.

It also frustrated her that she hadn't been smarter, more aware, more grateful.

"Olive?" Doyle said again, and she realized she hadn't answered him.

"Not now," she said, more because she didn't know what to say than because she couldn't have told him she wanted to go outside and talk.

She met his eyes again, deep, deep green, and felt the inexpressible shiver that went up and down her spine.

His eyes narrowed, but his gaze didn't move away.

She allowed her eyes to linger for just another moment, noting the square jaw, the sharp nose, the laugh lines at the corners of his mouth and eyes that didn't used to be there, before she turned, hooking her arm in the handle of the car seat and straightening back up.

Her eyes shifted back to his once more, even though she didn't mean for them to, and she caught the surprise, betrayal, the...hurt. She had hurt this good man, badly, and yet he had come to her, not with anger, but with curiosity, and...maybe even forgiveness?

But now, seeing the baby she held, the open expression in his eyes closed, and his gaze became guarded.

"Yours?" he said, low, under the murmur of the people speaking at the front of the church.

She nodded. Ashamed, but keeping her chin up. She'd made mistakes, a lot of them, but she didn't regret her daughter. Maybe she regretted the circumstances, regretted the decisions that led her to Ecuador and all of the things that happened there, but she could never regret her little girl.

Doyle nodded curtly, then, rather than turning and going back to his seat, he murmured, "Excuse me," and then walked around her and went silently out the back door.

She wanted to follow him, wanted to explain, to beg forgiveness, to make things right between them, but she wasn't sure that was possible.

Finding an open pew toward the back, she set her baby down, who was thankfully still sleeping, and slipped in beside her.

Livvy was a good baby, which was one of the many blessings that at one point in her life she might not have been thankful for, but she was so grateful for now. God had been so good to her, and she hadn't appreciated much of anything.

When she had been lying in her hospital bed in Ecuador, not sure whether she was going to live or die, barely conscious, and having no clue of who was watching her child, she had promised herself that if she got out of this, she would make a point to be grateful to God every day, for the many things that He did for her that she, up until that point, had taken for granted.

Things like waking up with no pain, being able to breathe without thinking about it, growing up in a small town in a country like the United States, which, while it was not perfect, was better than any other country she'd ever visited.

Better because of the freedom, better because of the open friendliness of the people, better because of the godly heritage she didn't even realize she rested on.

She hadn't been taught to stop and appreciate things. She'd been taught to constantly strive for more, like what she had wasn't enough, when it certainly was.

Although, right now it wasn't. But she'd cross that bridge later.

"I wanted to give everyone a chance to ask any questions they wanted to. So, we'll open the floor up for that right now."

The man at the front, who looked so much like Garnet, her sister Mertie's longtime childhood friend, that Olive couldn't believe it would be anyone else, stood at the microphone, one arm around Mertie and one around some young girl that looked like a carbon copy of Mertie beside him.

"I didn't think you were married. But your daughter looks exactly like Mertie Jardine. What's going on?"

From where she sat in the back, Olive couldn't tell who was speaking. It had been years since she had been back to Raspberry Ridge, and while she almost certainly knew the person, people changed, and looking at the backs of their heads didn't give her much of a hint.

But the question struck her, because the man was right. The little girl that stood beside her sister looked exactly like her sister, but as far as she knew, Mertie didn't have any children.

"Well, that's a good question." Garnet spoke, glancing at Mertie, who gave a small nod, before glancing at the young girl, who nodded as well. The girl shifted, slipping her arm through Mertie's, and Mertie reached over with her other hand, patting the girl's fingers and then holding them.

It was a sign of comfort and solidarity, and it made Olive smile to see it.

"Mertie and I are planning on getting married. I didn't mention this when I was candidating, but since the Bible clearly says that a pastor should be the husband of one wife, I wasn't going to accept the pastorate on a full-time basis if I wasn't married. That was just something between the Lord and me, something I knew needed to happen in order for me to be a pastor."

There were a few murmurs in the congregation, but most people seemed to be accepting.

"Mertie and I have decided to get married, and I've already spoken with Dominic, the head deacon. He has agreed that I won't be on full-time until Mertie and I have set a date and are actually married in the sight of God. We don't know when that's going to be, but soon." He glanced over at Mertie, and she gave him such a soft, sweet smile, so uncharacteristic of her commanding, in-charge, always-plowing-ahead older sister, that it almost made Olive tear up.

Would she ever give such a tender look to a man?

She glanced down at Livvy, sleeping quietly beside her. There had been no tender looks, nothing with the kind of love in it that flowed between Mertie and Garnet. Of course, Mertie and Garnet had always been friends, good friends, and now, with her travels under her belt, Olive thought that perhaps being friends was a prerequisite to being more.

She couldn't imagine getting married to someone she didn't like. Lust and like were two different things. She wished she hadn't needed to travel to Ecuador to find that out.

She wouldn't have minded if she had never found that out, and she wouldn't have, if she had taken what God had put right in front of her. Doyle.

"What about your daughter? Dabney?" the man reiterated.

"There are some things that we need to discuss among the three of us before I can answer the rest of that question. I know you understand. I'm not trying to hide anything, I just can't give some information out before certain things have been taken care of."

The man nodded, and then someone else said, "We might not have hired you if we had known you'd had a child out of wedlock."

"And that's reasonable," Garnet said, not seeming to be angered by the statement at all. "I feel like I would have been misleading you if I had not told you that I had a child out of wedlock. But I did not. I adopted Dabney when she was a baby, but I had nothing to do with her conception."

"You and Mertie were good friends. And that looks like Mertie's daughter."

Olive had come to the same conclusion, and after glancing around the congregation to see who had spoken, she looked back toward Garnet to see what he would say.

"We were good friends. We are good friends. And she does look a lot like Mertie. I promise, we will tell you everything, but there are a few other things that we need to do before we can do that." He lifted his brows. "Any other questions?"

"Are you going to go to the hospitals and do visits? Visit nursing homes? Work with us to figure out how we might be able to grow our congregation?"

Garnet started to answer, and Olive tried to pay attention, but her mind wandered, wondering where Doyle had gone and feeling bad that he had left what was obviously an important meeting for the Raspberry Ridge congregation.

The meeting dragged on, and Livvy started to stir.

She stood up, grabbing the handle to slip back out of the church, when her eyes met the eyes of a woman who had turned around. She was sitting beside a man, his arm around her shoulders, and he looked down at her as she turned.

Amara. Her sister. She recognized her almost immediately. And just after she did, Amara's eyes lit up with recognition, and she hopped a little in her seat, then turned quickly to the man beside her and whispered furiously in his ear before she stood up, walked in front of him out the end of the pew, and hurried back to Olive.

"Olive!" she said softly, but her voice burst with excitement. "You're here!" She went to throw her arms around Olive, but just at the last second, she saw the car seat Olive held.

Olive hadn't mentioned the pregnancy, hadn't mentioned the ill-fated relationship, hadn't mentioned all of her regrets, and had not mentioned Livvy.

In fact, the excuses that she had given for not coming to Raspberry Ridge sooner had been just that, excuses, most of which had not been true, which Olive hated. But she hadn't wanted her sisters to worry. If they had known that she was lying in an Ecuadorian hospital, near death, they might have tried to find a way to get down to her, and she knew that neither one of her sisters, with their high-paying jobs, would have time to do that.

"Let's go outside," she said softly, wondering if she could put Amara off until Mertie was with them. That way, she wouldn't have to tell the story twice.

But it looked like she was going to have to tell it to the men in her sisters' lives as well as her sisters, since both of them seemed to have gotten attached to someone since the last time Olive had seen them.

Amara nodded, some of the excitement slipping off her face and concern and confusion replacing it. But she waited while Olive squeezed out of the pew, which was thankfully still empty, and carried the car seat with an awakening baby Livvy in it to the back, slipping out and into the bright Michigan sunlight.

The lake shone, deep blue and sparkling in the distance. She always loved this view. As she took a moment to stare at it now, taking in a deep breath and letting it ground her, center her, it fixed her thoughts on what was important. God. Bringing glory to Him. Bringing others to Him. It wasn't about her. Whatever her sisters' reactions were to what she had done, she couldn't control them and didn't need to be worried or upset about them. She could regret her actions while admitting that she had determined not to do them again.

That she had changed.

"Whose baby is this?" Amara asked, as soon as the door clicked closed behind them.

"Mine." She knew that was going to open a whole plethora of more questions, but she still hoped to head them off.

"When did you have a baby? I didn't even know you were pregnant!" Amara looked at her in amazement. "It wasn't that long ago that we cleaned out the condo in Chicago. You weren't pregnant then."

"It was winter. I wore bulky shirts. Sweatshirts. Coats. You guys just didn't notice, and I wasn't showing that much."

"I guess I remember that. I remember thinking you'd put on a little weight, but I hadn't realized that it wasn't just a little weight."

"It's legit that you have questions, but if you don't mind, I'm going to assume that Mertie has the same questions."

"I wondered if she knew things I didn't, and she just wasn't telling me!"

"No. I haven't told either of you. There's...a lot we need to catch up on."

"Well, this afternoon seems like a good time to do it, although Mertie might be tired. It's a big day for her."

"What was going on?" She had assumed that Garnet had been sworn in as pastor, but why was Mertie up there with him?

"Today the church voted Garnet in as pastor."

"What was Mertie doing up there with him?" she asked as they walked down the steps and away from the door a little bit. She didn't think their voices would carry into the sanctuary, but just in case, it was better to be safe than sorry. Plus, she needed to get a bottle out of her bag since Livvy was starting to fuss.

"She and Garnet are together. At least, I think so. Everything happened so quickly."

"Then maybe we should just all have a get-caught-up session, because I noticed that you were sitting with a man I didn't recognize."

"Yeah, we'll definitely need a session for that. You aren't going to believe what happened to me, and I need some time to explain, because you might be upset at first." That was actually a relief to hear, that she wasn't the only one with news that might be upsetting to her siblings.

"After Mom and Dad died, I thought that we would be closer than ever. You know? I wanted that."

"I still want that! But it's hard to be close to someone who's halfway around the world."

"I'm here to stay. At least stay as long as I can get a job and support myself."

Amara stared at her, looking confused, then thoughtful.

Olive allowed the baby bag to slip off her shoulder as she set the car seat down and knelt beside it, digging in her bag for the bottle of water she kept there and the formula, grabbing both, and setting everything out to get ready to feed Livvy.

Sign up for Jessie's newsletter! Get a free book, access to exclusive bonus content, get fun and funny updates on her life on the farm and more!

A Gift from Jessie

View this code through your smart phone camera to be taken to a page where you can download a FREE ebook when you sign up to get updates from Jessie Gussman! Find out why people say, "Jessie's is the only newsletter I open and read" and "You make my day brighter. Love, love, love reading your newsletters. I don't know where you find time to write books. You are so busy living life. A true blessing." and "I know from now on that I can't be drinking my morning coffee while reading your newsletter – I laughed so hard I sprayed it out all over the table!"

Claim your free book from Jessie!